Honor
Land

R.S. Guthrie

Dedicated to:
Colonel Fred Taylor, Jr., USAF;
Major Phil Hoard, USAF;
*Captain Christopher
Ayoub*, USAF/USA (ret.);
and all of the
men and women
who've chosen to
be in service of
their countries.
There is no gratitude of words
alone that is worthy
of your sacrifice.

ACKNOWLEDGEMENTS

First, you don't write a novel about Wyoming and not acknowledge the genuine, unique, hardworking, tough-loving people of the land itself. I have many friends there still, both American and Native American. The latter know how I feel about history, but every one of you has a pride that no one will ever be able to take away. I say with the deepest respect: I admire you more than any group of people I've known. You are the toughest, hardest-working men and women and your love for Wyoming and the land I will never tire of witnessing.

To my proofreader, beta reader, friend, confidant, and most importantly to the book, an honest reader and commenter, **Gail Gentry**. You always have the perfect suggestions and your proofing is eagle-eyed. Your forthcoming novel will show the world how much talent you've been gifted.

To my wife, **Amy**, who has read every novel I write more times in full and in part than any other living human being, thank you for believing in me but most for being by my side. The further we get in this journey to that porch swing the more I depend on you and you have supported my dream from the beginning. I love you.

To bestselling author and friend, **Nick Stephenson**. You keep me on the correct road. Your advice is like gold bullion, your mind as sharp as any I know, and your work ethic and talent undeniable and amazing. Thank you for everything.

And **to the readers.** I've said it before but will continue to reaffirm it: you are the lifeblood to the writer. And for me, every letter, each word, all the pages—they are ultimately for you. When you humble authors by reading their work and further by telling others, you help the writer survive to write another day. You are so very much appreciated.

PREFACE

I don't normally write a preface to my books, but I recently had a reader pick up the second book in a series and read it first. She loved the story but felt she would have enjoyed it more had she known the history of the returning characters better. I thought that was fair—once a writer has eight or nine books in a series, perhaps the need to inform the reader they are picking up book number four or five becomes less important, but when there are only two or three in the series, I decided it would be the proper thing to do to let you, the reader (or potential reader) know that this is the third in the **James Pruett Mystery/Suspense** series, so if you haven't read the first one (*Blood Land*), or second (*Money Land*), you might consider it.

I do my best to give enough background story in any "series" book that a reader should be okay if they haven't read the prior book(s), but I wanted to respect the woman who took the time to comment enough to put this preface in book number three of this series.

In fact, my editor on two previous works, Russell Rowland, told me that Alfred Hitchcock distinguished Mysteries by two different styles. The first was the traditional "whodunnit". From page one the reader had no idea who the bad guy or gal was. I likened that to a boardgame of Clue. The second style he deemed "Suspense". That would be where you pretty much knew (or thought you knew) who did what, but it was the *getting there* and the twists along the way that made the read a good one.

I tend to write the latter. I love twists. I also love putting something right in the reader's face and daring them to

3

believe otherwise. Because of this, however, I do work hard to make each book in a series capable (hopefully) of standing on its own as best it can.

For me, as a reader—and being a character-driven author—it is the relationships I develop with returning protagonists, ancillary characters, villains, etc. that make me want to read the books in order.

Whatever your preference, I certainly hope you enjoy *Honor Land* as much as I enjoyed writing it. Cheers.

Rob (R.S.) Guthrie, 2015

"You're the fighter
you've got the fire
The spirit of a warrior,
the champion's heart
You fight for your life
because the fighter never quits
You make the most
of the hand you're dealt."

Dropkick Murphys,
Warrior's Code

Prologue

Posted: Wednesday, July 22, 2015 11:15 P.M. MDT
Wyomingnews.com

BREAKING STORY: FOUR DEAD. WAR HERO ARRESTED.

By Sloan Martin, Editor-in-Chief, *Tribune Eagle* and *Wyomingnews.com*

CHEYENNE, WY. At approximately 9:45 P.M. in downtown Cheyenne, four male individuals, whose names have not yet been released pending identification and notification of the family, were discovered, deceased, behind a local bar and restaurant. A suspect on the scene was identified and, after questioning, was arrested by Cheyenne police under a charge of multiple-homicide.

The alleged murderer has been positively identified by police as a local man: Kyle Vincent Yoder. *The Tribune* is reporting that Yoder was honorably discharged from the United States Army and returned from Afghanistan in December of 2014, after serving his fourth and final tour of duty.

While in service, Sergeant Yoder earned three medals of distinguished service: a Purple Heart, the Silver Star, and The United States Congressional Medal of Honor.

Please return for updates throughout the early morning hours, as further information is made available.

"The veterans of our
military services have put
their lives on the line
to protect the freedoms
that we enjoy.
They have dedicated
their lives to their country
and deserve to be recognized
for their commitment."

~Judd Gregg

Chapter 1

CHEYENNE CHIEF of Police, Ewan Wallace, stared in surreal confusion at the headline running across the top of *The Wyoming Tribune Eagle's* main web page that had posted just moments before. It was only the waning end of the *fourth day* of Cheyenne Frontier Days, 2015, and one of the most heinous crimes in perhaps a hundred or more years of history had defiled the celebratory event, more than likely irreversibly.

His mind was spinning like a lopsided top; *crimes like this do not happen in this town,* the voice in charge of keeping the toy twirling said to him.

Four dead.

Murdered.

Brutally.

Wallace had held back some information garnered the previous night, such as the fact that the victims were tourists. The officers at the scene, Wallace had already been informed, identified the victims by their state-issued driver's licenses:

John Jackson.

Trevor McGowan.

Gerald Dogan.

Michael Bennett.

All California licenses; all addresses in Santa Monica.

Two addresses. One shared by Jackson and McGowan, and the other by Dogan and Bennett.

No weapons had been witnessed nor found at the crime scene. Under the circumstances and at the direction of Chief Wallace, two Cheyenne police officers had taken Kyle Yoder into custody, reading him his rights and informing him that he was being arrested for the multiple-homicides. It would be a while before a clearer understanding of what had occurred in that alleyway coalesced, but until then, they had a strong suspect, and it was also safer for Yoder to be in custody than living on the street.

The district attorney would decide whether to prosecute based on the evidence, how many counts, and what the official charges would be. The empaneled Grand Jury would hear the evidence and either indict or not. Wallace's job was to maintain civility, protect the public—local and otherwise—and also to make sure the suspect's rights were preserved.

And there were *hours* of police work that were only just beginning: the taping of the area; the gathering of each piece of evidence, no matter how small or seemingly insignificant; crowd containment; media management; the interviewing of witnesses and suspect; family notifications—and that list was but the negligible tip of the proverbial iceberg. Before the night was over, it would take the entirety of the Cheyenne Police Department—every officer on and off duty, from Homicide to Intelligence to Special Victims units; uniformed personnel; off duty desk sergeants; Traffic Division; even the borrowing of several State Highway Patrolmen and the nearby suburban departments.

But when you got right down to it, whatever agencies or individuals were called in, the story would always be about *Cheyenne*, in the town where *his* was the face of low crime and where that cheesy Wallace grin plastered on billboards, promised all who passed them a quiet, decent, *safe* place to live.

Wallace loved Cheyenne. He'd never considered being anywhere else—he'd never consider *being* anything other than a lawman. He knew in whatever generation he had lived, he would have chosen the same path. Cheyenne and her history were in his and his family's blood and heritage.

The original township was, after a brief, rascally beginning, eventually a city that embraced society and regulation—changed by a reinvigoration of law and order that supported the idea that a conglomerate of civilization west of the Mississippi was not only possible, but also profitable.

And safe.

Such a notion, a hundred and forty-plus years earlier, flew in the face of the ruthlessness and villainy of the *Wild West*. And though at times dramatized, the reputation of an untamable, scurrilous land, where too often the law went unenforced and the meanest, hardest men defined "society" was not wholly unearned. Such men of the times gained notoriety through reputations of fierce violence, and those reputations eventually made it back east to the "civilized" folk of the period, through handbills, news reports, and wanted posters.

Even in Cheyenne, an encampment that first sprang to life at the intersection of nowhere and the transcontinental railroad, as the young city grew, it became somewhat of a cliché of the *Wild West* legend: burlesque theaters, and rowdy bordellos and saloons to entertain the railroad workers, soldiers from nearby forts, horse regiments, and more than a few hardened types up from Texas, Arizona, and the rough men who rode west from bordering South Dakota.

Cheyenne was, for two decades in fact, nicknamed *Hell on Wheels*. Like many towns of the Old West, it could easily have succumbed to the times and devolved into just another place far too rough and dangerous for decent people to come, make a living, or raise a family.

But as the axiom of progress requires, there are visionaries who see beyond the adverse patina of a town, recognizing the inherent worth behind the crusty exterior; seers and dreamers who sense the profitable gem inside the lump of grimy coal.

Cheyenne's location was *premium*; the land on which she lay was in line with a critical, healthy artery to the east, and the cattle grazing ground went on for hundreds of miles—as far as the eye could see— and there was even more prairie beyond the mountains westward.

Money from early cattle barons and investors did finally make its way to the town, where those men of vision invested in the promise of moving livestock from the wide open prairie of Wyoming on the magnificent rails of the transcontinental—and then still *other* entrepreneurs realized the benefit in reforming the town from raucous, lawless, disrepute—monikers of some of the West's more infamous towns such as Dodge City, Kansas; Deadwood, South Dakota; Tombstone, Arizona; or Eldorado Canyon, Nevada—into a more sophisticated city, where opera, fine, luxurious hotels, and plush theatres with current productions, could thrive, bringing more and more people from the eastern seaboard.

To the futurists, Cheyenne was central to the entire country growing westward, and to those who had the means and turpitude to invest in such a venture, the upside was without limit.

And so, over the years, the cattle barons *did* stake their claims on land, raised herds, shipped beef east and, eventually, west to the miners in California. Fine hotels and good theatre *did* bring the cultured folk from the east, and the largest opera house west of the Mississippi was built.

Hell on Wheels was replaced by *Live the Legend of Cheyenne, Wyoming.*

And the people came.

But none of it was sustainable until Cheyenne's first police department was formed, and, more crucially, *maintained, reinforced, and given real authority.* Too many ventures into the untamed west had failed—failed when the towns meant to sustain civilization, rejected it instead. The legend of Cheyenne could only be brought to reality by fearless lawmen, and commensurate investment in an enforcement agency determined to ferret out ruffians and scoundrels and those who had learned in other places to spit on the law.

The cattle barons and entrepreneurs who turned the fortune of Cheyenne, Wyoming, might not have been any less greedy than their predecessors might, or of those that would follow them over the decades, but they foresaw that without *heavy investment* in law enforcement, too, there would be no legendary city along the transcontinental.

So the Cheyenne Police Department was formed, and slowly, resolutely, the law was laid out, enforced, and since there were many other unscrupulous towns from which to choose, the bulk of the bad element bid farewell to Cheyenne, and *Living the Legend*, to which the city's motto was shortened, became a real possibility.

Chief Ewan Wallace's great-grandfather, Otto Wallace, was one of the first (and finest) officers of the Cheyenne Police Department, eventually rising to the level of Chief of Police, as would two of his progeny. And it was under the watch of Chief Otto Wallace that the motto of the police department was formed:

Protect the Legend.

The mission statement, as it was, stuck. But over a century later, it wasn't Otto, but, rather, *Ewan* Wallace, who faced the biggest challenge of his career.

In a city where crime was low, people trusted each other, and where the seriously bad news normally occurred elsewhere in the country (or world), a bona fide nightmare had fallen flat into the center of his beloved jurisdiction. *And* on the fourth day of the city's most famous, prideful, ostensibly *enjoyable* event.

In other words, a variation on disaster:

SNAFU—Situation *nonstandard*, all fucked up.

Fortunately, for Wallace, he'd grown up smothered in an atmosphere of law enforcement—father, elders, brothers, uncles, and even a sister—all sprouted from the roots laid by lawman Otto Wallace.

Unfortunately, Ewan Wallace had been born chubby, without coordination or instinct, and was the unofficial black sheep—and dark little secret—of the Wallace clan.

Still, any man raised in a family so steeped in the bylaws of duty and protection and service could not help but be taught certain inalienable lessons; one being how to simply go into *cop mode*: suppress panic; focus on the situation at hand; consider the options available—regardless of how limited—and, most crucial of all, rely on the wisdom of the *system*.

One of the first lessons a police officer was taught remained standard throughout the decades—regardless of size, severity, or circumstance, still, at its core, *a crime was still just an act*—and there were procedures to be followed for every type of illegality.

As bewildered as Wallace might feel, if he stuck to doing what he'd been trained to do—if he stayed calm and implemented procedure, based on the rote driven into him by his training and by soaking in all that legendary family law enforcement over the years— then he'd be fine, and he could attend to the protection of his city, talent and backbone be damned.

At least that's what he told the fear rising inexorably inside and prayed it was true.

Murder was murder; Ewan Wallace had been a soldier (though perhaps not the finest or bravest—even war had its share of "timecard punchers"), but more importantly he had trained near boundlessly for a moment like this. That it should come then, in 2015, or whenever—it was a crime, on his watch, and he was the Chief of Police.

That should mean something aside from the romanticism and the history and the honor about which Wallace enjoyed rambling forth after a few beers; it should mean he had risen to his place because of his ability, his fortitude, and his experience as a police officer.

Was that true? Wallace had wondered before if he was yet another example of benign incompetence, rising higher and higher in a broken system, as if political helium (the hot air of ladder-climbers, kiss-asses, coffee-guzzling committee organizers, and kowtowers to the almighty bean counters), rather than competence, lifted too many men and women higher and higher in the "chain of command".

In the end, Chief Wallace decided, whatever truth prevailed, it could not be changed, and it seemed perhaps the questions that plagued him on those sleepless nights—the demons and secret apprehension of the self—would all have their answers, one way or the other.

Chief Ewan Wallace's true mettle would be put to the test.

He would solve the biggest crime in his career. Or at least that is how the news reports would spin it. Ewan Wallace was not preparing to call the best cop he knew out of the camaraderie bursting in his heart. The man was a friend, but more crucial to Wallace, he was *good*; and if a politician was what Wallace was at his core, then knowing whom to call to make the chief look good was an elemental skill. Find the man with the necessary courage and detecting skills to ensure that the crime of the century be solved and that when that fact was announced, Chief Wallace could take as much a bite of the credit pie as he wished.

He couldn't allow the cops that caught the case, Wilkins and Burnstead, to solve the crime—not that they likely would; not in the statistical forty-eight hours—but *if* they somehow stumbled into an answer, Wallace knew that Wilkins was upwardly mobile. That boy would milk the cow on all four teats, leaving Wallace looking like the flat-assed paper-pusher up in the ivory tower.

No, there was something about this case that was not right—that much Wallace's own gut told him—and whether it was ferreting out the true killer or killers or whether it was not allowing any mistakes to give the current suspect any chance to slip through the system, well, it would take a special kind of man for such an appointment; it would require an outstanding law officer that, as good as he was, wanted even that much more to stay out of the limelight and shirk the credit.

Wallace knew a man like that.

The murder happened downtown, District One, so the case was caught by the detective team of Charlie Wilkins and Greg Burnstead, two seasoned CPD detectives, first grade, which traded twelve-hour tours with two other District One pairs of Homicide detectives.

Wilkins and Burnstead were on duty when the tourists were killed, so regardless of the numerous departments, jurisdictions, and agencies that were assisting with the myriad moving parts of the investigation, their team was lead.

While patrol officers canvassed the downtown district looking for anyone who had seen or heard anything, Winston and Burnstead interviewed the only known witness, Chip Kaczynski, who was also the 911 caller. Kaczynski was a bar-back and sometimes-bartender at the overflowing bar, Whiskey Pete's, downtown.

Actually, all the bars in downtown Cheyenne during Frontier Days were overflowing—the city had an annual moratorium on their normal open container law, allowing the crowds from the numerous downtown bars to overflow into the streets, which were cordoned off from 7:00 P.M. until the bars closed at two in the morning. The crowd noise made hearing the commission of a crime less likely, but the sheer number of people in the area at the time offered hope that the uniforms would find someone else; perhaps a less-willing witness to the murders.

Chip Kaczynski was out in the alleyway behind the building for a smoke when he noticed several bodies on the ground, spread in a semi-circle, twenty or thirty feet down the asphalt, toward the dead-end.

A black and white brought Kaczynski to the station to give an official statement.

"Tell us again," said Burnstead to the witness. "From the beginning."

"Man, this is a huge bummer. I've told this story three times already."

"And you need to tell it again," Detective Wilkins told him. "I know it sucks, but we have four dead bodies, Chip. You can appreciate the fact that we're no happier than you, yes?"

"It's going to be *tomorrow* soon, and I haven't slept in twenty hours, fellas."

"You keep up the sob story, *fella*," said Burnstead. "You'll be lucky if you get any for another twenty hours." His role as bad cop was well deserved. He never minded putting the screws to a suspect, or a witness, as long as he felt information was being suppressed. Wilkins' role was less *good cop* and more *handler*, keeping his partner on the leash, pulling back when necessary—and Burnstead relied on it. They were a decent team. "Talk. To. Us. *That* is your way out of here quick and tidy, Unabomber."

"Unabomber?"

"My partner has an embarrassing habit of making up monikers. Plays on people's names, the way they look—you know: fat, thin, same name as the Unabomber. Department shrink says it's not unlike Tourette syndrome. Thing is, the nicknames, they get worse the more you antagonize him," said Wilkins. "I've seen him make hardened criminals beg him to just, for the love of God, STOP."

"Fine," relented Kaczynski. "For the fourth time: I went out for a smoke, saw the four guys—the victims—lying on their backs. I walked down to see what gives and saw none of them was moving. Then I saw the fifth guy, just sitting there, you know, a few feet away. He had blood all over him and looked like he'd taken a few punches himself."

"No one else on the scene?" Wilkins said.

"No."

"What about Front Street?"

"Shit, man, you know Front Street. It was packed. But there wasn't anyone I saw back in the alley. Just me and the dead guys. A- and the suspect, I mean."

"What do you mean exactly by 'anyone I saw'? That's not the same as you said before," Burnstead said.

"What's the difference?"

"You tell me. Did you see anyone or not?"

"No. I didn't see anyone else."

The big cop looked at his partner. "Why don't I believe this guy?"

Wilkins shrugged.

Burnstead slid his chair around the table and pressed in tight with Kaczynski. "If later on I find out you were withholding information, I am going to make it my personal goal before retirement to put a bummer down on your life so hard you're gonna *wish* you were only the Unabomber."

Kaczynski had started shaking. "P-please. Can I get a smoke?"

"Sure, you can have a smoke. *When you start telling the truth, Unabomber Boy.*"

"O-okay, look," Kaczynski said, Burnstead still no more than an inch or two away from his face, looking as if he wanted nothing more than to be left alone with the scrawny man. "This chick. Allison. We're, uh, well, we're friends kind of."

"What the fuck is 'kind of' supposed to mean?" Burnstead barked, Kaczynski squinting and retreating ever so slightly at each punctuated syllable.

"W-we sort of—we dated. For a while. She works the busy months, summer mostly. Look, she's twenty. I didn't, don't, want to get her in trouble."

"We're not interested in busting underage barmaids," Wilkins said, still standing near the door. Burnstead hadn't moved an inch. "What's her last name?"

"Chapman. Allison Chapman."

"And what were you and sweet Allison in Wonderland *doing*," Burnstead asked, his irritation piqued.

"She was with me. For the smoke."

"Before or after you?"

"W-what?"

"Did I fucking *stutter*?" Burnstead said, slamming one of his slabs-of-meat hands on the table.

Kaczynski jumped half a foot out of his seat and for a moment, looked as if he would start crying right there. "Before, before. She was out there a minute or two before me, I think."

"What do you mean 'you think'," asked Wilkins evenly.

"I, uh, saw her by the back door around nine-fifteen. When I looked again, and she wasn't there, I figured she'd gone out back for a smoke, so I followed her."

"So you can't say for certain *when* she went outside," said Wilkins.

"I guess not for sure."

Burnstead finally leaned back, put his thick arms behind his head, and interlaced his sausage-like fingers. "He guesses not. Well, I'm satisfied."

"Also, uh, she didn't go with me when I walked down to see what had happened at the end of the alley. She said her shift was over and she went toward Front Street. Disappeared into the crowd."

"And you thought a shift ending at 9:30 P.M. on one of the busiest nights of the year—a time of year by your own accounting was *when she worked*—was routine?"

"No. I mean I was focused on the guys down the alley. I really didn't think about it until now."

"I don't see *thinking* as your strong suit at all," said Burnstead. "If I were you—and sweet Jesus I'm glad I'm not—I'd cancel any applications for international think tanks and whatnot and stick to stocking coolers for the drunks."

"And you didn't see any weapon?" said Wilkins, walking around the small room, behind Kaczynski.

"No, man. I *swear.* No weapons anywhere. I told everyone that asked. There was no weapon."

"That you saw," said Burnstead.

"T-that I saw."

"You ever hear of a charge called 'delivering a false statement'?" said Burnstead. "How many times you complain earlier about having to tell your story?"

Kaczynski wisely remained silent.

"Three times. Three times, you said earlier. We could charge you right now—right here, right now. You could do time, Unabomber. And I could let my sources inside the penitentiary know that you're related to the real Unabomber. I'll let 'em in on the fact that you were your uncle's errand boy. You know, running around, getting him shit to use in blowing up good, hardworking Americans. You know who hard cons like just slightly more than pedophiles? *Traitors.* Or is it less, Charlie? I can never remember which. But they'd take a real interest in *you*. Hey, maybe I could tell them you're a *pedophile* traitor."

"Oh, man," the young man wept. "I swear to God I don't know anything else."

"You give us a minute," said Detective Wilkins.

The two detectives stood in unison and left Kaczynski at the interview table. In the hallway, they compared thoughts.

"You were a little hard on the kid," said Wilkins.

"Guys like that make our jobs ten times harder than they need to be and *I'm* being too hard? Nah. Being too hard would have had to include something physical, like a cuff in the back of the skull." Burnstead's demeanor had completely ratcheted down.

"Not an unfair point."

"We need to find this Allison Chapman."

"Sounds like she might be in the wind," said Wilkins.

"Let's get an address from wonder boy in there and cut him loose for now."

"Yeah."

Burnstead led the way back into the interview room and returned to his chair, only a foot away from Kaczynski. He smacked down a small, spiraled notebook and a cheap pen. "Write the address down," he snarled.

"A-address?"

"Of the Queen of England, you stooge. *Your girlfriend.*"

Kaczynski grabbed the pen and scribbled an address.

"We better find her," Burnstead said. "Now get the fuck outta here. And stay in town. Don't make it hard for me to find you."

"No, sir," Kaczynski said and slipped past Burnstead as if he expected a boot in the ass on the way out.

"Have a nice night," said Wilkins.

~

"So do you want to take a run at Yoder now or go find the girl?" said Wilkins.

"Let some uniforms go check her address," Burnstead replied. "If she's there, have them bring her in. If she's not there, and we're not getting anywhere with Rambo in there, we can go looking for our phantom second witness. You agree?"

"Mainly because we may not have time with Yoder. Wallace called earlier and left word. His arraignment is at eleven tomorrow."

Most murder cases—a solid eighty percent—would go unsolved without a concrete lead in the first forty-eight hours. Once Yoder was in the court system, even just for a preliminary arraignment, the detectives would lose access to their prime suspect for at least the day. Maybe two.

"I'll go call dispatch and have them send a car over to Allison Chapman's place," Burnstead said. "With any luck, they'll find her there and we can get outta her what she saw or didn't see, *and get it tonight*."

"You mean *this morning*."

"I have a feeling we're not going to know the difference for a while on this one, partner," said Burnstead, and patted Wilkins on the shoulder as he walked past. "Go talk to Yoder. I'll be back in a bit."

Kyle Yoder had been cuffed to the table in his separate interview room for at least two hours, alone, no water, the air intentionally turned off. The man looked to Wilkins as if he'd just been escorted in and sat down. He hadn't changed his position at all since they left him in there.

Yoder didn't move or acknowledge the detective entering the room. He'd not asked for an attorney, but technically, he had not agreed to any interview—he had literally yet to say a word since being arrested. Or before that, as far as Detective Wilkins knew.

Kaczynski, in his statement and in subsequent interviews, had reported that the suspect was nearly catatonic when he found the man, staring at the ground, mumbling gibberish.

"Anything I can get you?" Detective Wilkins said, sitting his tall, lean, muscular frame into the metal chair across from Kyle Yoder. "Something to drink?"

Yoder offered no response. He was wearing a dirty Army jacket and jeans; clothing the cops had allowed him to keep to wear after bagging the bloody shirt, pants, and all his other possessions. He clearly hadn't been shaving regularly, or showered in some time. His hair was past shoulder length and his beard was substantial. He looked twice his twenty-three years.

"My name is Detective Charlie Wilkins. My partner, Greg Burnstead, will be in here in a short while."

Nothing from Yoder.

"Let me explain the situation, Kyle. Thing is," Wilkins said, "one way or the other, we know what went down last night, out in the alley behind the bar. This is *fill in the details* time, that's all. If it went down like self-defense, or for another understandable reason, this is the time to say so. No one is here to find out if you killed those four men. We know you did. And when the forensics team is finished with the evidence, they'll reconstruct the scene, and you'll still be sitting here, silent, and they'll say what we all know; they'll have the *evidence*, son."

"I'm not your son," Yoder said quietly, nothing but his mouth moving a millimeter.

Wilkins felt the shock of the suspect speaking creep across his face, but Yoder never would have seen it. He remained fixated on a point somewhere beneath the one way mirror, on the peeling paint of the lime green wall.

"Fair enough," said Wilkins, happy enough to have gotten the man to start talking about anything. "You're not my son, that's correct. I apologize. But we *have* gathered your known history, Kyle. We know what happened to your parents. Doesn't make for an easy beginning."

Yoder looked up, moving only his eyes. He locked on Detective Wilkins' baby blues. There was no emotion behind the opaqueness of Yoder's brown eyes; they were not dead, exactly, only devoid of answers—they promised only one thing: they would divulge nothing. Not ever. "I didn't have a poor childhood. I wasn't mistreated and I wasn't made to feel fatherless or abandoned. And even if I had, I wouldn't blame anything from then until now on it."

"So what, then, makes a man like you kill four innocent men? Something set you off."

Kyle Yoder moved his gaze back to the same spot on the wall and said nothing.

"Now's the time, Kyle. You can sit there and wait for them to take you down and charge you. But I am trying to be straight with you here. It's not like any of us can make past bad shit go away, including what happened tonight, but you can do yourself some good here. Tell me your side. It will help. I've seen it a hundred times before."

"It's not up to guys like you," Yoder said. "You can't make that kind of call."

"No, it's not. But guys like me get to talk to the people who *do* make the decisions. Don't kid yourself, Kyle. Four charges of homicide, *that's* the train coming down the tracks, and you're right in the middle of the rails right now. You don't give me some reasons, there won't *be* any more *listening to your side*. At that point, the evidence will be speaking *for* you."

"I think it may be better if I wait for a lawyer."

Just then, Burnstead burst in. He sat in a third chair, scooted it noisily over to the side of the table, closer than Wilkins.

"Man, you smell, son," said Burnstead.

Yoder looked up.

"It lives," the detective said.

"You can mock me all you want," said Yoder, no longer looking at the detective.

"Yeah, you're right, war hero. I *can* mock you. Look at yourself. How do you get up in the morning? Guys like you who try to live forever on the accomplishments of yesterday make me sick."

The suspect remained silent.

"You getting anywhere with Rambo here?"

Wilkins simply shook his head. They were in a dangerous area now. Wilkins knew Burnstead had been listening. The suspect said the word. Lawyer. He hadn't yet fully asked for an attorney—but it was a very thin line the detectives were walking. If the suspect *did* give them anything useful, there was a chance it could get tossed.

Wilkins decided to follow his partner's lead. It was a judgment call, but the cops could make a solid argument that Yoder was not clear in his decision to wait for an attorney.

"Big hero," Burnstead said, keeping his opponent off balance. "Why don't you do us all a favor and confess. Jail seems like it would be an improvement over your current circumstances."

"Do yourself some good, Kyle," Wilkins said. It felt as if there had been progress before, miniscule as it was; he did not want to risk losing even a shred of rapport.

Detective Burnstead slammed his hands on the metal table. He stood and leaned in real close, so he could whisper. "You don't impress me. You don't scare me. I'd like a few minutes alone with you, cameras off. We'd find out who's the hero and who's the piece of shit killer."

Wilkins put his hand on his partner's shoulder. "Go grab some coffee."

Yoder had not reacted at all to the detective's taunt.

"Fine. You keep dancing with him," said Burnstead, and walked out.

"I'd apologize for my partner but, well, he is who he is. Like the rest of us, I guess."

Yoder still said nothing.

"In a few hours, you're going into the court system, Kyle. Once the district attorney makes the charges a part of the official record, there won't be any going back to the opportunity right here, right now."

"This isn't going anywhere. We want different things. You want me to give you information and I'm not going to give you any. So, with all due respect to you, Detective Wilkins, you can go out and tell your big, mean partner behind the glass that I am officially availing myself of my right to counsel. I'm done talking or answering any more questions."

This time Yoder's eyes rose ever so much and locked with the reflection in the mirror.

And whoever was standing beyond.

"We must be willing
to get rid of the
life we've planned,
so as to have the life
that is waiting for us.
The old skin has to be shed
before the new one can come."

~Joseph Campbell

Chapter 2

Three Days Earlier

JAMES PRUETT returned home from his big meeting and as he walked past the unopened bottle of Heaven Hill bourbon in the center of the kitchen table, he set his five-year sobriety chip atop the cap. Scattered at the bottle's base were a handful of different colored chips: a one, three, and six-month, plus his one, two, three, and four-year chips.

Like birthdays, Pruett was to the point where he'd rather not be reminded of the years as they passed; even the sober ones. He felt good then. In control. He wasn't naïve enough to think he was cured. That would never be the case. He just wanted to stop thinking about it.

And so he had. The meeting tonight was more for the others; those men and women who had yet to receive a chip; those who had received them, at one time, but had fallen backward, beginning again.

He did it because it was the right thing to do.

There *had* been a time when he'd felt by keeping the bottle there, he was facing down a gladiator, morning after morning; evening after evening. It was two years into his sobriety that he decided the booze before him had no honor and was not worthy of his comparing it to a gladiator of old. Gladiators had honor; they fought for their lives because they had no other choice—but they kept their integrity. The booze had neither honor nor integrity. And when he had drunk it, Pruett had no honor either.

Now his mornings began with a jog around the property line, a light bit of circuit training in the basement, and then a tall cup of dark-roast coffee.

Sober.

After Bethy was gunned down at her own family's property, continuing to be the sheriff had been his purpose. It's what saved him that night; it's what kept him just strong enough to live through the funeral and the burial and the nagging, never-ending realization that he would be alone inside himself forever.

He would just keep on being sheriff.

And he did. Going on six years. During which time he'd even fought off the damned Mexican drug cartel, by god.

Saved the town—*his* town.

But all that was gone—history. Washed away as quickly as the flash flood of water and mud and deadfall debris roared past, destroying every living and nonliving thing in its path.

The events of late had tested his resolve, enough raw shock that it should have caused him not only to *fall* off the wagon but to leap from it at a hundred miles an hour. But the temptation was not as incontestable as he feared; it seemed he'd become stronger than he realized over the years.

Either that or the shock was so large that even his unquenchable dependence for alcohol was dumbfounded and feeble before the most recent bombshell.

He still couldn't believe it; not even three months later.

He was merely James Pruett.

Not *Sheriff* James.

Just *Pruett*.

That's all he was now. Voted out by his own people. He'd not believed anything could tear his soul in two as the death of his wife had six years earlier. But life didn't answer to the plans or the expectations of humans.

Not life OR God.

Especially Bethy's and his father's God, the one Pruett also, if he were being honest, believed in, too—even though He hated Pruett so much. Seemed to the ex-sheriff, anyway, that the Almighty was intent on punishing him for whatever sins he'd committed—intent on his being under attack for the rest of his days—even though Pruett could name three dozen people in Wind River alone that were more deserving of the treatment of Job than he, if that's how the system worked.

But he'd learned to accept that reality, too. There was no system. Pruett decided that being punished some certain number of times wasn't the point. Once wasn't enough. Not twice, nor three times, nor four.

There was no number. No maximum. No minimum.

Penance. It covered a LOT of territory.

And there was no medicine for it or amount of ruin or sorrow that would balance the scales, so Pruett had long since decided it was a fool's errand to try. The debt, he realized, was being brought into the world, like it or not. Life. And the liability was not payable in advance; the only payment that would be accepted was the cost every man and woman owed: one death.

And all the penance that could be stomached (and then some) from cradle to grave.

The rest, however, knowing the rules, was what one made of it. So a man like Pruett could choose to mold his life into a monument of sorrow or a statue of gratitude for all the good things.

Hell, ten minutes with his Bethy would have been worth a lifetime to Pruett.

Then he looked across the room at the revolver, his first gun as sheriff, slung over the back of a dining room chair in its well-worn holster. There was still just one cartridge chambered. Hollow-point bullet. Too many times he'd stared down that single bullet. Every morning and night for a year.

When he lost Bethy, he'd wanted to end it: the day she died; after the wake and funeral; when he finished burying her.

Then every time he thought of the cold covers on the other half of the bed or the empty chair on their front porch.

Because it wasn't about the alcoholism or the lonely days and nights or the aching hole inside him that nothing could fill—it was about needing a reason to keep on keeping on.

Being sheriff had been Pruett's reason for getting out of bed.

There *had* to be a purpose.

For him—for everyone. What use was a life lived if nothing was ever accomplished? If being on the planet for so many decades amounted, in the end, to having nothing left to keep you going, *why keep going?*

At that moment, the ex-sheriff wanted to eat that bullet far more than he wanted a drink. (Well, were he being honest, a nice double shot of Heaven Hill before blowing off the top of his head would probably be the most reasonable failure imaginable.)

But he'd become too strong for that. Too wise.

Yes, Pruett had gotten complacent; believed that for the rest of his days, being sheriff would be his purpose. And now, even though he wanted no booze, nor to die just yet, he didn't know what he was going to do.

Surviving the worst thing that can happen to a person changes them. Not in the cliché manners that most would think—oh, for the weakest on the food chain, that was it: they crumpled into the fetal position and spent the rest of their days finding more terrible ways to crawl toward an unremarkable death, at least of the mind and soul, if not the body.

But those with backbone—people with a core necessity to survive even the most abysmal of circumstance—they soldiered on. They crawled up from whatever godforsaken hole into which they'd been thrown to suffer and they crept along until the inches equaled a foot, and then the feet equaled a yard.

Ultimately, it would have to be one step at a time; just like getting sober. He'd have to rise every morning, put his feet on the floor, run his run, drink his morning coffee, and then, well, then he would figure out what to do.

And once the first day was complete, he'd start it again. But with another ounce of purpose. Maybe with the beginnings of a plan.

The key was in getting back up.

Yet there was one difference this time than all the rest of the times he'd taken the punch, hit the ground, and gotten back up.

He wasn't the gladiator anymore; he wasn't the caretaker or the hero.

He was just James Pruett.

James *fucking* Pruett.

Deep inside him, quiet for a time, the ogre again stirred.

Tough talk and thinking was easy. Action took balls. Withstanding the seductive promises of the beast within—or worse, climbing back into the ring, yet again, standing toe-to-toe, punch-for-punch, with the experienced brawler.

And if Pruett stood there, unmoving, frozen with indecision, steeped in self-pity—if all he cared about was a *literal* hunk of metal; a manmade badge of honor—he would eventually fall. He'd tear that paper seal, spin the bottle cap, and throw back a double-shot of the deceitful elixir, and the beast would howl in victory.

The beast was fully awake now; it growled surreptitiously, placated by a moment of potential weakness—grateful to be aware and in the game—and Pruett knew the creature awaited his next choices with the sharpened eye of the chess master.

Pruett had discovered that in such moments, whether in true battle or simply the war with the self, man would either succumb or triumph. Regardless of the size of the skirmish, those were really the only possible outcomes. Win or lose; eat the bear or *be eaten*.

Experience showed him that, for a man like him, either outcome was a possibility. But if Pruett gave in, he wouldn't take just one drink—there would be another, and another, and he would eventually lose count, until his eyes became long, horizontal slits in a face that already looked as if it had been pounded out of dark, aged leather, wrinkles running like spider webs across his countenance.

It came down to a question without complexity: *was he finished?* Beaten down so hard and stomped on so many times that getting up just wasn't an option anymore? He thought of Ty McIntyre in that moment; Ty, the bull rider.

How many times had a man like McIntyre pulled his broken body off the ground, not asking anyone for a hand or for anything else to assist him?

A man could get up and limp away if there was something to fight for—something worth the countless, unknown days ahead. For someone like Ty McIntyre it didn't take much, maybe, but for Pruett, he needed days that would not be filled with the shame of no longer being who he'd always *been*.

How had he lost something that he'd felt was a part of him? Something that would define him for the rest of his days? And what did he do now that the definition was gone?

At that monumental moment of crossroads, Pruett thought back on days with his father, Michael. The preacher had been hard on young Jimmy Pruett in many ways, and as most children, Pruett had not understood him then. But as he grew into manhood—as the childlike things were put away—much of the hardness toward his father, and even some of his father's stern lessons, softened.

It was exactly for a time like this, decades later, old then himself, that he realized he needed the presence of his father—or at least the lessons from the man—the most.

Pruett ignored the bottle on the table. Instead, he walked out to the front porch, leaned on the wide, flat pine rail, and sucked in a long breath of fresh, Wyoming air. So many times he'd turned to the infinite stars of the Wyoming night sky and wondered if his old man was up there.

He moved over to one of the two chairs, his chair, and sat. He bent over and put his face in his hands. *So much*, he thought. *So much TIME*. He felt as if he'd lived forever. Pruett sat up and contemplated the heavens.

As if in tacit agreement, the beast inside did not make a sound; rather, his mind took him back to a day his father had taught him one of the hardest lessons.

During the sermon that particular Sunday, Jimmy Pruett and a few of his friends had been poking each other and giggling quietly in the rear pews while the elder Pruett boomed on about God and the calamity He poured down on His servant Job. Several times, young Jimmy Pruett stole glances at his father and didn't see anything that would lead him to believe they could be heard.

After the service, Jimmy was not called ceremoniously to his father's office, and on the drive home, his father had even caught Jimmy's eye in the rearview and smiled warmly.

They had been home a good hour when Jimmy's father asked him if he wanted to go fishing. There was a slow rolling stream twenty yards wide that snaked through the Pruett property, and Michael "Preacher" Pruett was known countywide as the worst fly fisherman God had ever seen fit to put on the earth.

Still, Pruett's mother would make ham and mustard sandwiches and a thermos of flavored fruit drink and father and son would hike down to a spot in the river where the water was so clear you could toss a dime or even a dark penny and see it sitting amongst the rounded stones on the river bottom: two, three feet deep.

The water was more clear than glass and deep enough that they did not have white water, and Pruett's father would choose a spot where the river bent and he could cast his chosen fly out where a crafty rainbow or brown trout might be hiding away in a shadowed spot too far into the bend to see the man and his pole casting for dinner.

Sometimes his father would catch a fish, but most times, he wouldn't; yet whatever the take from the river, Pruett remembered *always* hankering for those ham and mustard sandwiches on wheat bread, cut into perfect wedges for eating, and the sweet, cool, flavored water as it washed down each bite.

Most of all he remembered enjoying the talks he'd have with his old man—they weren't meant as sermons: no booming rapture with fire and brimstone and terrifying horses with riders named Pestilence and War and Death. They were more like even-spoken lessons, for Jimmy only—private tutoring from a much-respected man who tutored an entire community every Sunday morning.

That one particular day, however, after the sandwiches and other items were made and placed in the Army-green backpack Jimmy would sling over his shoulder, his father told him to meet him back at the toolshed and they'd walk to the river from there.

When Jimmy arrived, he immediately saw his father's thick, brown, leather razor sharpening strap, and when Preacher Pruett motioned for his son to set the backpack aside and bend over, the boy's bladder nearly gave out.

"You know what to do," his father said, not in a mean way, like some times, but in a matter-of-fact tone. "And you know why you're doing it."

Those whips that day hurt more than Pruett could remember any hurting him before or after, and he'd been strap whipped across the buttocks more than a few times in his childhood. His father was no abuser as such—he did what parents did then; they delivered lessons, sometimes with the switch or the hand or the leather strap instead of only words.

That day, Pruett's father gave him three lashes; two that hurt like Hades, and one that was so brutal Pruett, the man, still bore the scar.

After the whipping, Jimmy Pruett picked up the backpack and father and son walked to the river as they had a hundred times before (Jimmy with a bit of a limp, but he'd hiked to the fishing hole that way before, too).

Later, when eating the delicious sandwiches after an unsuccessful fish, it was silent but for the small breeze whispering through the willows and the trickle of water over stone. It was a perfect moment, but all Jimmy Pruett could think about was his sore behind.

"You didn't think I heard you boys making that ruckus in the rear pews, now did ya?"

"No, sir."

"Felt like you got away with something, not getting called into my office after the services or scolded on the drive home, didn't it?"

"Yes, sir."

"That's the way life is—they call it *complacency* or sometimes *taking things for granted*." He chewed on a fresh bite of ham, mustard, and bread. "Doing something bad isn't the real issue, James. Far worse is that feeling you get—that comfortable notion that you'll just sail through the rest of the day, doing normal things like fishing, eating sandwiches, and it seems like nothin' is different than it ever was."

Pruett had nodded, the automatic reaction of a child yet unsure of the lesson's message (and still fretting over the burning sting across his backside).

"I wanted that whooping to come outta nowhere, son; meant for it to catch you unsuspecting."

"It did," Jimmy Pruett responded, quite honestly.

"I'm sure it did, boy. In life, we start feeling like we get away with things—maybe not one particular thing or another, but just all of it, like maybe God isn't watching, and then it begins to feel like just because we don't get caught, what we did isn't *wrong*. We'll wake up every day, just like all the rest, and everything will be just fine; our parents will be there to love us; we'll play marbles or buy ice cream or pretend to do our homework.

"Point is, son, we get to feeling pretty good about ourselves, and that feeling becomes our normal, and that's called getting *complacent*.

"Yep. Complacent. It's a bit like your mind just taking days off. Goes on autopilot.

"And then, from way out in left field—BAM," Preacher said, and Jimmy had leaped nearly an inch off the ground, almost dropping his sandwich in the stream.

"Maybe a car smashes into you; or a tornado tears down your home and everything that ever mattered to you like it was all just made of matchsticks; or cancer strikes down someone dear to you, without warning or mercy. It comes outta nowhere, son, just like when you thought you were fine, today, having goofed off through an otherwise majestic morning."

And then the boy had grasped a part of what his father had been driving at. And in the present—a much older James Pruett—understood fully the gravity of complacency.

People let their guard down. They let a rosy complexion and a strong gait hide the fact that a dark sickness could still be growing inside. They—HE—let the fact that a wonderful, innocent woman who had nothing to do with a roiling family feud would therefore be safe, each day as the next.

Pruett went back to the table and picked up the bottle. He pressed his thumb against the seal until he could just hear it beginning to tear.

The gladiator wasn't the booze. And neither was Pruett—though he had been once; had been many times, in fact. And it wasn't his own constituency that cast him away.

It was complacency.

The true enemy; the enemy of the gladiator.

A person got comfortable with himself—taking his successes and happiness and clear skies for granted. As if no storm could gather itself up along the prairie horizon and come roaring into town to destroy every man, woman, child, and building.

Or wipe away a career.

James Pruett wasn't sheriff anymore.

They voted him down.

Complacency didn't vote. It was his own people; his surrogate family.

They'd taken back the shield of the gladiator, but they'd done it because he hadn't proven himself worthy any longer.

He eyed the gun again. It was no gladiator either; just an inanimate object without a hero or villain to wield it; an object of molded steel without thought, or will—even without the ability to act unless it was picked up and brought to bear by a person—someone alive, breathing, sweating, and *feeling*.

Someone with *intent*.

But as a gun could be commanded to carry out the will of its owner—even an owner who had lost his way, his will, and his purpose—such truth didn't make the weapon any less capable of doing what it was made to do.

Gladiator or not, the man who wielded it—hero or foe—could *kill*.

James Pruett had once believed that a man should be able to wake each day and look into the mirror—into, as Nietzsche had said, the abyss. But what Nietzsche *didn't* say, or, perhaps, didn't *contemplate*, was that a man staring into the abyss might find the abyss not looking back into him at all, but rather just inanimate blackness, *the abyss finding nothing in the man worth considering*.

Ex-Sheriff James Pruett poured the bottle of artificial courage—an abyss and a crutch for five years—into the sink. The pungent, yeasty smell made his stomach spin and growl and slash at his innards like a crazed wildcat.

James Pruett picked up the retired sheriff badge and his sidearm.

It was time.

Pruett walked into the Wooden Boot to find Sublette County's new sheriff, Jake Walker—not a child, Pruett was continually forced to remind himself with palpable effort, but rather, a man, albeit one of barely thirty-one years. Walker was sitting where he always did for morning coffee: at a table where he could see all the pretty waitresses shuffling around, their butts pointed mostly toward him, since he was at the front—amongst the "self-seat" tables—where the servers less-often attended.

Pruett shook his head; he fought back the irk he felt at the boy's youthful predictability as well as an urge to slap the hat off the little bastard's head. Pruett could teach him several lessons in one physical act: keep your back to the wall, not the windows; stop chasing skirts on duty; and, perhaps most sacred in Wyoming, *take your fucking hat off inside an establishment.*

The latter was grounds on more occasions than one to earn you a mouthful of fist on a drinking night. The ex-sheriff did not give in to his instincts, however, or, rather, he allowed his *better* instincts to take control. Pruett had not come there for trouble; just the opposite, in fact. He figured if Jake Walker was going to hold the position of Sublette County Sheriff, and considering the reality that Pruett still loved Wind River and wanted to see her well-protected, the situation called on him to be the bigger man.

Pruett also figured he owed a measure of respect outright, because of Jake Walker's roots. Most folk in Wind River had ancestry there, and just as you didn't judge bushels of apples by the one or two uglier pieces, you didn't judge a family history—earned as honestly as any other—by one or two persons that happened to stroll the wooden sidewalks with the same surname as another.

The Walkers had been in Wind River for as many generations as Pruett remembered, or had been told, and the bulk of them had always held positions of honorable service: in the school system and the church and other various professions, organizations, and committees. Many even served in public office.

Yet as personally accurate as was Pruett's rationalization, his own feelings for Jake Walker were not kind, nor were they without merit. Still, as duty and appropriate behavior suggested, the old man remained respectful of the long, honorable Walker family history in what the ex-sheriff still considered "his" town.

That said, and internally, where the score mattered most, Pruett could *not* put down the notion—nay, the *reality*—that the boy had been, and likely always would remain, a blight. Self-serving, arrogant, misogynistic, and perhaps even a tad racist.

Yes, there were more than a few negative adjectives, but Pruett still preferred *blight.*

It played well with the apple analogy.

He watched the boy for a few moments before approaching, as any good lawman would, ex or not. And as if to punctuate the true character judgment of the man who was now only *James* Pruett, the newly-elected head of Wind River law enforcement showed his cliché card by leaning over and taking a peek upward one of the younger waitresses at the Boot.

Pruett once again suppressed a desire to handle things the way they might have a hundred or so years earlier and continued the high road. Still standing just inside the doorway, he slowly removed his Charlie 1 Horse hat, walked deliberately, boot heels clicking, in front of the boy—blocking his view for a few tactical moments—and pulled over an unused chair.

The ex-sheriff sat at the same table as his replacement, uninvited. Some habits of engagement, even if rude and/or otherwise purposeful, would never be discarded. Not in the rarely changed repertoire of James Pruett, anyway.

Yet before either man could say a word, Pinky Vandersloot, sixty-something, skin crinkled like a lost edition of last January's weekly fish-wrap and sporting her trademark, heavy, bright pink lipstick, called out:

"Coffee. *Black*, right, Sheriff?—" Pinky looked as if she'd sucked a pea down her windpipe and the color in her cheeks washed past her overdone makeup. "Uh, apologies. *James*? No offense," she added, directed toward Jake Walker, but without that ring of sincerity.

The black coffee comment was a long-standing, if somewhat tired joke. The excusable faux pas of calling out his previous position, however, did ruin the delivery on that particular occasion, appropriateness notwithstanding. No one in the Wooden Boot noticed—other than Sheriff Jake Walker, of course—whose bristled ego tickled Pruett's pride.

"No offense taken, ma'am," said Pruett, offering an old friend forgiveness for the misspeak *and* acknowledging the joke, all in the same response. Pinky Vandersloot seemed to recover somewhat, and winced in an aged smile.

Pruett looked across the space at *Sheriff* Jake Walker—he still could barely *think* the words, much less say them—wondering if the young man might offer the lady even the slightest smile of thanks or affirmation.

Walker offered nothing.

Pruett groaned inwardly and, with perceptible effort, left the moment in the rearview. Keeping the conversation between just the two of them, he still tried a ham-fisted verbal attempt at breaking the ice and erasing the uncomfortable silence:

"You just can't help wondering how many men have at least once in their lives gone home with those wide, telltale pink tracks up and down their prized possession."

"Huh?" said Walker.

"Never mind," Pruett said, already sorry enough for the stupid attempt to feel his own brand of shame. "You're a bit young to get the reference. Mind if we talk?"

Pruett didn't wait for an answer, turning the chair backward, out of habit or intent he couldn't say.

"Look, Sheriff—uh, *Mr. Pruett*," Walker stumbled, choking on his *own* misspeak. "If you came here to poke fun at my age, or debate me like you did during the election—"

Pruett was already waving him off.

"Sorry, Jake. No, not at all. Scout's honor, Sheriff Walker."

"Now, see; it's sarcasm like that gets me riled about your intentions in sitting down with me."

"Not said with sarcasm, Jake. Just a mouthful for me at the moment. Such discomfort will pass with time, I promise you."

"I hope so," said Walker, fidgety; perhaps, Pruett wondered, not comfortable yet himself in full uniform.

"I'll let you in on a bad joke from days past—it is about as appropriate as Pliiky's coffee comment, though that truth doesn't dissuade the lady from returning to it whenever I come by on a particular morning. Let's just say she's got a reputation that began quite a while before your time. The whole moment was lost in translation, I think. All the way around. I meant the acknowledgement of your office full of due respect, not sideways— even if it may have sounded that way, I mean."

"Fair enough," said Walker.

"Sorry I busted in on your breakfast coffee. May I stay a bit?"

"Only if the visit's friendly."

"Yep. Total truce," Pruett said, and smiled with honest warmth.

"If you say so," said Walker, clearly still not convinced.

"Now, see," Pruett said, his anger again beginning to glow, like the embers of a fire that were blown on a bit. He stopped; counted to three in his head—as Jesse, his sponsor, had taught him to try—and was able to contain himself. "Okay, here's the real deal. It ain't easy for me, Jake. Maybe if you were closer to my age, you'd understand. A man serves as long as me at *anything*, it's going to take a while before he can face up to a monumental change. 'Specially one that's more like a gut punch."

"Uh-huh."

"I'm here as friend, not foe. The election is over. I know I didn't take it well. And I know people around here—some of them— have not made it easy on you. Folk in places like Wind River don't adjust quickly, or necessarily easily, to change."

"What exactly is meant by the lecture?"

"No lecture intended. I already told you, I wasn't here to talk at you sideways. Yet you as well as anyone also know that I am a man to speak my mind; not one to pamper you with false assurances. Your office may be one of majority vote, but the *responsibility* of that office is *not*."

"It's a different time," Walker said, looking past Pruett. "Vote said as much."

"Let's give each other the respect of recognizing the razor close shave of those election numbers."

"It's not my fault the campaign to get out the younger voters worked, even in a small—. In a small town."

"Hick is what you thought to say, ain't it, son? Hick town."

"What I think isn't your concern, Mr. Pruett. Fact is, however close the margin, I won the election. Maybe we're just seeing the town and its requirements through two different perspectives. Not one right and the other wrong necessarily; just *different*. Times do change."

"Perspective and times changing are both good and well, Jake. But no matter how you view Wind River, you're not only here, but you're the sheriff of *here*."

"Meaning?"

"Meaning this town depends on you now. The whole county does. From every rancher to every teacher to every member of the county commissioners."

"Implying my uncle had anything to do with how this all turned out?"

"Not in the least. Last I checked, every man, woman, and child in this country is free to speak their piece about who they stand behind. I mean everyone now depends on you, Jake."

"If so, it'd be nice to hear 'Sheriff' more often in your vernacular."

"I've been to college, too, Jake. And you'll have to forgive my *vernacular* if it's a bit slow on the change. I mentioned before, it'll get there. But I'm not going to beg you to take my olive branch."

"Guess I can be the aggressor, too," Walker said.

"Here's the thing, son. What you said about things and places changing and all that? It's not wrong or inaccurate. Wind River has changed a lot over the past ten or twenty years. Hell, just the gas boom alone changed the face of her from a dust bowl with one stop sign to an actual stoplight on the state map. But being a cop? That's not about veneer or appearances. Not a whole lot changes in the human race, no matter how many new storefronts go up or how many stoplights get put in a township. Not over a hundred years, much less a few."

"And you think I don't understand that reality?"

"I think you're a smart man, Jake. I do. But yeah, I think you need to take a closer look at what you've sworn to protect. It's more than the face of the town; you owe her to cover everything that comes with the package."

"I studied law and criminal justice in school, sir. I think I know—"

"That's just it, Jake. A good investigator has to know what he *doesn't* know; and he needs to be able to test the wind and get a feeling for anything that might not walk right out and bite him on the ass."

"So now it's about my skills as a cop?"

"Studying criminal justice and the law doesn't put you into the job with any more experience than the next person, Jake. I'm here to tell you that where the books leave off, you can call on me if you need to."

"Message received, Mr. Pruett."

"I hope so, Jake. I really do. Being a good cop and protecting your town, well, it requires you to be a step ahead—especially with those you perceive as adversarial, right up front—and you need to read between the lines."

"Meaning I can't? Or aren't, anyway?"

"Meaning if you begin by stirring every man's hornet's nest whenever you get a bit rattled, or especially feel you're the one being attacked—"

"Now wait a minute—"

Pruett put a flat palm in space. *Time to shut up and listen to the old man.* "See, you *think* you are not antagonizing the situation. Maybe you even think your icy stance equates to toughness and gives you the upper hand. What I'm attempting to impart is the experience that you can learn a lot more by staying out of the fray rather than jumping right in—wait out your adversary a bit, let him do the talkin'. It's one tactic that can work, anyway."

"I thought you weren't here in an adversarial capacity," Walker said.

"You missed the part about perceptions," Pruett said. "But since you brought it up, as sheriff, you need to be aware that any situation might turn that way, regardless—and maybe especially—when it's been stated otherwise."

"So in-between those lines," Walker said, "I'd say things are potentially moving toward the adversarial. Or that's the hint?"

"Nope," said Pruett. "No hints. No games."

"And no threats?"

"Jake, I came here in a right mind, and with decent intentions. That this conversation maybe took a left turn where I intended a right, for that I apologize. I truly didn't intend that."

"Apology accepted," Walker said, the intensity ratcheted down a notch or two.

"I sincerely meant to send some hard-earned experience across the table and hope that you use it if or when necessary."

Jake Walker looked thoughtful after Pruett's final remark. Something must have settled in, because he lost that look of a fighter scanning the crowd for a scrape, and he nodded tentatively.

"I appreciate it," the younger man said. "But like you, I guess I'll have to ask for time in coming to terms with our common interests."

"Fair enough," Pruett said. "That's all a man can ask of another."

"I honestly appreciate the neutral talk, Mr. Pruett."

"Tell you where we can start this tenuous partnership. Mr. Pruett was my father, and if you think dealing with me is hitting the rough seas, you'd not have wanted to meet him. You call me James, Sheriff Walker, and we'll go from there."

"Thanks, James. I appreciate any advice you can give me; anything to help me out in my new office."

"You're welcome, straight up. And I'll work on getting used to using your new title."

"Hell," Jake said. "I called you 'Sheriff' myself. This town has had Sheriff Pruett overseeing it since I wasn't even a thought in my father's head; I know that—and I respect it, too. More than my detractors know, in fact. And that's straight up, too. You call me whatever you need to call me. And whenever you want to."

"I appreciate it," said Pruett. "I'll get there, son. I believe in the office you hold; that means I need to believe fully in you, and fully support you, too. That's one of the three things I came here to tell you."

"Speaking of noticing things, I *did* see when you walked in that you're carrying a loaded Smith & Wesson on your hip."

"Funny thing, this town," Pruett said, a bit more sardonically than he intended. "You remember ten, twelve years back, all those national news crews—all four, plus CNN, so I guess it was *inter*national—came scooting up here just because somebody dug up an old law that still says it's rightful for anyone to carry a loaded weapon into any establishment, as long as it's in the open and the owner's got no rule against it?"

"Yeah. I was in college; all my roommates called me down to the community television for me to see my hometown."

"Make you proud?"

"Not particularly," Walker said, the look of awkward shame crawling across his face. "Kind of embarrassing."

"You remember the most embarrassing part?"

"Who could forget? Butch Keller standing in front of the world, dressed head to shiny silver boot toes in black leather—shit, that fool even had on *spurs*—barking like it was the Old West up here. People watching—my friends, even—thought Wind River was Tombstone. After that interview, the next three tourist seasons folks came here expecting real gunfights in the middle of the street."

"Brim Butch, we've always called him," said Pruett, grinning. "Or just Brim, mostly. Because he was always full to the brim with booze and bullshit, both, always."

Walker laughed, the tension between the two nuzzling itself down some more.

"You know who owns this place, right?" Pruett said.

"Hell yeah," said Walker. "Never gave it much thought. Butch—uh, *Brim* Keller."

"Yep. Point being," Pruett said, smiling, motioning to his sidearm, "I'm both availing myself of my lawful rights and protecting myself from that nut bag."

Walker smiled. "Makes sense to me."

"Didn't come to shoot you, is also what I'm saying."

"Glad for that," said the new sheriff, just as Pinky Vandersloot finally brought Pruett his coffee.

"Hot and black," she said for at least the hundredth time in Pruett's lifetime. "Just how I like 'em."

As much comfort as old things remaining the same gave him, the energy consumed by Pruett's sucking in of pride—holding back myriad words that he *wanted* to say but didn't—and his generally chronic condition of alcohol thirstiness, didn't leave him with the amount of requisite grace when it came to dealing with a kind but loony citizen like Pinky.

Still Pruett maintained his exterior composure. Internally he was less successful. Her unintended callousness didn't bother him so much as did her damned *ignorance*.

How'd you like it if I mentioned we also used to call you 'Puffer Vanderslut'? Pruett pondered, but did not say, keeping his cool yet again. He simply thanked the old lady.

Pruett's internal machinations apparently went unnoticed, as Jake Walker sipped his own coffee, cream, and sugar. When he spoke, however, it was with more deliberation:

"You said something about 'three things' you came to say. You've only hit on one."

"Yep," Pruett said, and sipped at the hot brew. "Second was something I should've, but never said. And that's a sincere congratulation for winning our election fair and square."

"That means a lot, Sheriff."

This time Pruett knew the title didn't slip out.

Good for you, kid.

"Well, I mean it," Pruett said. "On the heels of that, the last thing is, since I *have* been overseeing Wind River for a stretch, I want you to know that any advice—ahead of time, under fire, whatever— is offered freely, honestly, and without duress. And I'll do my damndest to have your back."

"Thanks for that, too," Walker said, smiling warmly for the first time. "To be honest, I was hoping you and I would get to that stage one day. I'm not going to lie and say I couldn't use your years of know how and experience."

"Well, son, you got it. Any time you need it." Pruett put out his meaty paw and Walker accepted it, the thin bones in the new sheriff's hand mashing and crinkling under the thunder grip of the ex-lawman. "Wind River should be our common ground, if nothing else. I'm with you on that one, Sheriff Walker."

"I'm glad. And what you might not know is that I love a good poker game. Texas hold 'em, truth be known. I've heard you and the deputies have a semi-regular gathering. If you're ever missing a body, or otherwise need a player, I'm in. Not saying I'm a shark, but I can hold my own. Thought maybe such a gesture might loosen up the team. Start to build some camaraderie."

"Noted," said Pruett, and actually meant it. In addition to being a truly good idea, as far as teambuilding went, the old man had financed two new fishing rods the previous year on his winnings from cards. Fresh meat was always welcome to the slaughter.

"First piece of advice," said Pruett. "I'm not going to be calling every week, so I figured I'd try to summarize the one thing I'd leave as a takeaway. Exude confidence, son; right from the first meet. Never assume what you're walking into is anything like what it appears, or that who you meet is what you expect. You start there, be fair, and you're going to make a good lawman."

"Thanks again," Walker said.

"You're the *sheriff* now," Pruett said. "The badge will earn you *some* respect, but the rest, it'll come off your lead. Serious as Satan, here, Jake. Just work on it. You need to be in command of every situation. Like it or no, first impressions are big amidst our particular tribe."

"Okay."

Pruett threw back the rest of his coffee like a shot of Heaven Hill. "Kind of a bonus gift, in parting. Going to offer you my professional services—investigation, data dissemination, people finding, missing animals, whatever might be the issue at hand. Decided last night I can't stay busy fishing only. I'm taking over the old Mountain Vista Realty building on the town square."

"The place across from the courthouse? You going into selling real estate?"

"Nope. Just need the office space. Hanging a shingle as a private investigator. Already applied for my official license, have the carry and conceal permit—though you can see I've never been the concealing type. I'm just about ready to open the doors for business."

"What—?"

"Here's the thing I can't decide," said Pruett, standing up, putting on and adjusting the Charlie 1 Horse hat atop his considerable dome, and smiling sardonically, waving his large hand before him, as if he could see the sign itself:

"*James Pruett Detective Agency* or *Sheriff Pruett Investigations?*"

It was the first time throughout the visit that the youthfully self-confident Walker became childlike and silent.

"It's kinda like ex-Presidents," Pruett said as he walked past, patting Walker hard on his thin shoulders. He looked across the room and tipped the brim of his hat to Puffer.

He winked at Jake Walker, Sublette County Sheriff.

"You still have to call them *Mr. President.*"

"Commitment is an act,
not a word."

~Jean-Paul Sartre

Chapter 3

Eleven months earlier;
Nearing Election Time

AS PRUETT wrapped his thick fingers around the cold, sweating glass of sweet tea with lemon, he stared at them. They made him look so old. He *was* old, but his hands were unlike the rest of his external; the hardness of each year showed in them, the wrinkles like the rings of a tree or strata in the earth. He studied them, lost in trance— copious, heavy strands of used up rope, so aged they seemed to have already carried or raised all they could, and just might not hold together for any more tasking.

He was at the Wooden Boot—every night, the darkest bar in Wind River, Wyoming, patronized by workers from the oil patches and gas fields and by the most hardscrabble men in town. During the day, it was also a good place to grab a quick coffee or breakfast, and then lunch until the midafternoon.

Pruett had always liked it there—did his best thinking sitting at the bar, even when he was sober, as he was now, and had been for over four years. Some people worked out the knots in their brain best in a hot, soaking tub; some while they ran a spirited loop around a park in a thriving, early morning city; some on the john.

Sheriff James Pruett had always felt most unwound, clean-slated, and peaceful of mind there—in the roughest bar in town. He'd thought many times about the irony of a drunk—a *recovering alcoholic*—finding a bar one of his happy places; one of his most comforting places on earth. And Pruett had to admit to himself that it *did* surprise him that he could still come there, year after year, and remain sober. Perhaps the Boot and he were made for each other, in that way that every man needed a place to take off his hat, rest his legs, and feel un-judged.

And by then—after four years of sobriety—he'd finally trained the bartenders. After more than a few false starts, they now knew how to make him his new drink: the perfect ice tea; with lemon slices, two packets of raw sugar, and a spritz of soda put in a tall Tom Collins glass—too tall and thin to swig, it allowed him to drink the cold, refreshing elixir of his sobriety in tiny, mindful, appreciative sips.

Pruett had found that it was the smaller things in life that could pacify a needy soul: a tall, cool, sweating glass of goodness, plate of lemon slices, and a basketful of raw sugar packets. Not that strychnine crap that had an aftertaste like the sweat-soaked inside of a shoe. The real thing. Real sugar sweetened the tea just so, taking the sour from the lemon; and the concoction was as close as Pruett had found to the drink Bethy used to make from her fresh sun-brewed porch tea.

It seemed silly to want things just so, and usually the sheriff didn't—he wasn't the anal or particular type—but as he got older he did find that he preferred routine more and more and detested surprises.

So there he sat, cold condensation running over his fat, rope-like fingers—the glass sweating almost as much as Pruett was from the nerves inside his gut. In another ten or fifteen minutes his two deputies (and one ex-deputy) would arrive, coming there because he'd called them and asked them to; asking them there because he needed to discuss something with required honest consideration, but was the last thing in the world about which he wanted to engage his team.

"More tea, Sheriff?" Bonny Elder, the barkeep, asked him with a purposeful, quarter-grin on one side of her mouth.

"Bonny, you been serving me here for the better part of eleven years. And it's been nothin' but tea for at least three or four. It's just *now* you're gonna start teasing me about it?" Pruett said, smiling coyly.

"I tease you about it all the time, you just don't listen. Lost in thought, I suppose. You treat my flirting the same way."

Pruett smiled big. "Yes, then, please. On the tea. We can discuss the flirting another time."

Bonny smiled fully. "Now that's a promise I'm going to have you sticking to."

Bonny Elder had always held a bit of sway over Pruett. In his drinking days—decades earlier, when he wasn't as clear about who he was and who mattered to him most—he'd kissed her one night as she was closing down the bar.

It never went further than that (mostly because Bonny wouldn't allow it—not with Pruett being a married man), but he *had* offered to walk her to her car; an offer she'd coolly declined, and ever since, there was a space between them.

Still, as if to prove that all things change with time, over the years since Bethy's death and since Bonny had lost her husband of then, twelve years, to cancer, that space had slowly grown more warm than chill.

"That, I will," said Pruett, and meant it. "But for the moment, I'm going to move over to that round table in the back corner. Some friends are coming to see me in a bit. Figured I'd grab us a spot."

"Yep, the place will be filling up soon for lunch," Bonny said as she walked down the length of the bar to make his drink.

Pruett moved to the far table, back to the wall, and wondered how well he would deliver the words to his team and if they would make a difference. The old sheriff liked things thought out in front of him, ready for the next evolution.

Hope for the best; plan for the worst.

Pruett didn't know who had said it, or if it was just a maxim of the universe, but it was how he lived most of his life—the parts he'd kept within his control, anyway. And it was now he felt the department should prepare for the worst. Otherwise, he and his deputies might find themselves caught in the headlights of the oncoming train, frozen, unequipped to deal with the locomotive. As Sublette County Sheriff, Pruett could not afford to allow for that prospect, regardless of his own pride or circumstance. The well-being of the town came before anything, including Pruett's oversized ego.

He surveyed the room of mostly empty tables. He'd always been drawn to keeping his back to the wall, even as a child. And his idiosyncrasy had not gone unnoticed—neither when he was a child or an adult:

"Sheriff Jimmy Pruett," his father would say, meaning to compare him to the television Westerns of the day rather than forecast the future. "Back always to the wall where he can spot the scurrilous villains before they see him first."

Truth was, Pruett had never wanted to be a cop, not until later, after the war. Maybe the instinct had always been inside him and he'd just not recognized it. Hell, as a child Pruett thought he was going to be starting middle linebacker for the Chicago Bears—each week praying they'd be on television and *in the afternoon game,* after church services, so he could cheer and marvel at Dick Butkus, number fifty-one, the visceral, cunning, beast of a man who looked as if he could take on the entire opposing team himself just by staring them down with his intent.

Pruett could not remember having any other ambitions or career intent—only that he would never follow in his old man's footsteps. No preacher was James Pruett, and when the local boys in Wind River made the mistake of trying on *that* particular nickname, they paid the price of poking the bear.

"Sheriff Pruett," said a familiar voice, tearing him from the thoughts of times past. Once-deputy, Zach Canter, arrived first and removed his jacket before accepting the bear hug offered by his former boss.

Canter then lived in Cody—having left the department almost a full year prior—and was co-owner of a restaurant he ran with his father-in-law. He was in town for the weekend; one of the reasons Pruett had scheduled the get together.

"Figured I would find you in the rear, back to the wall, where you could cut down a whole room of quick-draws before they had a chance to fire a shot," Zach said, a huge white-toothed smile across his face. "I've missed you, sir."

Pruett smiled right back, trying to keep his emotion roped and secured, lest he let loose and blubber in front of his friend. "Damned good to see you, Zachary. Is being the restaurateur everything you wanted it to be?"

"It's not bad," he said, sitting down next to the sheriff. "Actually, it's more work than I ever imagined it'd be, but I truly do love it."

"I'm happy for you, son. Even though you're sorely missed around here."

"Heard you haven't hired my replacement yet, though. Been almost a year."

"Some things are difficult to change," said Pruett. "Plus the damned county commissioners hold on to every penny in the budget like it was their own personal funds they were spending. Said they'd think about backfilling the position next year."

"After the election?" said Canter. The kid was nobody's fool.

"Yeah," said Pruett. "After the election."

A flash of sadness ran across Zach Canter's face and was gone as quickly as it had appeared. "Sounds about right," Canter said, ordering a glass of water from Bonny Elder when she brought Pruett's tea, plate of lemons, and basket of raw sugar.

"Ah, the county commissioners wouldn't know their own assholes if you bent 'em around, shoved their faces up to the pucker, and gave 'em each a flashlight and a magnifying glass."

A few minutes later, Melody Munney and Red Horse Baptiste arrived. Only Munney was in uniform, like Pruett, on duty. There were the perfunctory hugs and handshakes with Canter, then small-talk banter while each ordered something to drink or eat.

"It's good to see the three of you together again," Pruett finally said, after some appetizers and drinks had arrived. "It truly is."

The rest of the table raised their glasses and tipped them toward their sheriff.

"You're each smart enough to know there's always something behind me puttin' together a meeting like this—a luncheon, as it were."

Munney raised her hand. "You all know who usually gets *that* duty," she said. "You old misogynist."

"I won't deny it," Pruett said. "The socialite in me, well, there really never was any socialite in me."

The table laughed in unison.

"Thing is, I wanted to talk to you as a group, and I didn't want to do it down at the station." Pruett motioned to Zach. "I also wanted you here, son. You know it'll never be long enough for me to think of this team as not including you."

Melody put her arm around Canter's shoulder and Red Horse Baptiste nodded, stoic as ever.

Pruett continued. "Goddammit, I wish we were here for fun times, or at least better news."

"What's wrong, boss?" said Baptiste.

"Nothing wrong," said Pruett. "I invited you here because I need you to each make a promise to me. I don't want any arguments or debate. This isn't just for me it's for the entire town."

"Anything," said Canter.

Munney and Baptiste simply looked straight at him. Their loyalty was without question and required no words.

"I want you to stay on as deputies with the department when I lose this upcoming election."

Present Day

Cheyenne Frontier Days is an event that has been described by one writer as "a glorious, contemporary mixture of the Old West, current Wyomingites, curious tourists, the younger generation, and an opportunity—regardless of age, background, or source of frustration—to forget about what ails you for a time, join with your fellow humans, and come together for nothing more than one universal ideal: the embrace of old-time revelry."

There are others, young and old, who see it as it can appear from the outside: an excuse for drunks of all size, shape, and manner to drink. And drink. But it is a celebration of all things Western; one that has occupied a ten-day period of time somewhere around the final dog days of July, for over a hundred and sixteen years.

Beyond the inevitable partying in town at night—and there *was* a lot of partying downtown at night—the event had grown to draw nearly a quarter–million visitors to a city with a listed population of fewer than sixty-thousand residents.

It is by far the largest single annual tourist attraction for Wyoming, Nebraska, *and* even Colorado to the south. Being ten days long, there are myriad concerts, daily rodeos, air shows, free pancake breakfasts, western reenactments, and even a Pamplona-like "Walking of the Steers": a kickoff, three-mile walk into Frontier Park to await the forthcoming rodeo events.

Kyle Yoder had seen more Frontier Days than most, having grown up in Cheyenne. The majority of those had been spent in his youth—young men and women using whatever means they could to forge their age so as to enjoy the nights downtown, a deception that was easier when the drinking age was nineteen.

Even for locals, however, and excluding the businesspeople counting on the density of tourist traffic over the two-week period, it was a time of year to be anticipated and enjoyed with enthusiasm.

2015, however, was a different year in more ways than Yoder could remember—more had changed than just his apathy at the approach of the city's most honored celebration. The most difficult evolution was his honorable discharge from the Army—moreover, Delta—and his permanent return home from Afghanistan.

He'd begun his homecoming with an attempt to move in with his grandparents, an arrangement that lasted for only a few weeks. His best friend from high school, Stephen Archer, offered Yoder a place to stay for however long he needed, in a boxy spare room of Archer's small, downtown apartment.

Yoder's buddy had, when Yode joined the Army, accepted a scholarship and played Division II football at Wayne State College in Nebraska, gained his MBA at the University of Colorado, then graduated the culinary arts program at Auguste Escoffier School of Culinary Arts in Boulder, Colorado, hoping to open his own restaurant one day.

While Yoder lived with him—again for but a few weeks—Archer was then head chef at a nice downtown Cheyenne restaurant. The two talked about the war some, though Yoder found his ability to maintain conversation, particularly with civilians, was limited at best. Speaking about the war was even more challenging, especially since there were few specifics he could offer his friend even had he a desire to share.

Eventually he packed his necessities, thanked his old friend, and left to find somewhere else he could clear his head. Yoder was well aware that his inabilities to adjust to any of the well-intended offers of living arrangements back home were *not* the fault of the people who cared for and about him; it was *not* the fault of those who opened their homes to Yoder. The fault—if there was any—would be his alone to bear, though his departures hurt his family and friends, leaving them bewildered yet, he hoped at least, understanding.

Post-war re-acclimation would be a process, as it had been for every war and for every veteran; the unwritten code amongst vets was *to each in his or her own way, in their own time.*

Since returning from the war, even after the accolades—which included both a Silver Star and the Congressional Medal of Honor for saving eight trapped soldiers plus three more on the way out when running into hostile resistance—Kyle Yoder did not feel proud. It wasn't just that he felt out of his element, or lost in the "real world"—although he *did* feel those things; he was a Special Operations soldier who *was* different because of his training and his actions—an oddity even within his own community of regular soldiers.

But he did not feel left out, or without options.

There were more than a few privately-funded and public companies that had use for his particular skill set—many of his comrades had turned to them for post-service sanctuary; an occupation where they could maintain the level of intensity and tempo they'd grown not only to accept but that became, over time, *a necessity.*

But not for Yoder. He was done. His service to his country had been satisfied within him; his goals had all been accomplished. That he was now left with an emptiness that confounded him was, he supposed, not an unusual or unheard of condition.

And he was not crazy. He didn't know if he had PTSD, or at least he'd not been officially diagnosed with it before being sent back to the States. It was difficult to imagine that not all soldiers had some form or another of unmanageable stress upon returning home. Regardless of the crinkled, well-read letter from his godfather, Sheriff James Pruett, that Yoder still carried—still read each night before sleeping—he doubted that any human could survive war without wounds, external or internal.

Yoder did have a serious physical injury, received in his first and only engagement as a D-boy: he'd taken half a dozen rounds that day and two had shattered his left knee, beyond long-term, sustainable repair. The Army physicians told him he'd always walk with a limp, yet Yoder had refused even a cane offered him back in

Dubai. He conquered his rehabilitation as he had all other goals and challenges in his short life.

Then, back in the States, even in Washington D.C. getting V.A. assistance for anything seemed to be more trouble and paperwork than it was worth. He'd learned in Delta training to fend for himself under much more unforgiving and bereft environments than the city of Cheyenne. So he returned to the west.

Even at home, however, Yoder could not explain—for himself or to any Army shrink—what exactly was "wrong" with him. The best he was able to summarize was to say that he felt *disconnected*.

Not specifically from his family, or his friends, or even his comrades. He didn't feel specifically disengaged from any one group or individual. It seemed like he'd lost the ability to relate to the whole human race.

And whenever he would attempt to explain it to someone, the same look of horror would drop like a death shroud over their face, and he would assure them that it sounded far worse than it was.

He harbored no anger or resentment for anyone, least of all the people for whom he'd risked his life so that they could go on living their *normal* lives, free to complain about the government, the war, and yes, even men like him. He enlisted, trained, fought, and endured under no delusions, because of his own desire to serve the country and people he loved.

He'd simply found upon returning home that his love had turned to apathy.

Yoder, of course, had worried that he was suppressing something; one awful thing or another that would one day rear its head and then—hopefully without incident or bloodshed—he would *know*. But he did not feel like he was hiding or suppressing anything. Until he could reconcile who he used to be with who he was, he just needed time alone, with himself, to sort out what had happened to him.

And so, by choice, he took to the streets. Not because he was unsupported, as were too many of his brethren, but because it suited him. Yoder found a measure of solace surviving on his own, as he'd been taught.

A soldier and his gear.

Spartan existence.

To him (and likely to any Special Forces soldier), it made perfect sense. So despite the feelings of some of those closest to him, he made the choice he was built to make.

And he knew his evaluation of the situation was perfectly sane. He wasn't confused about his situation or circumstances. He knew the difference between the streets of Cheyenne and the mountains of Afghanistan—the difference between wartime and peacetime, as the one Army shrink who spoke with him for ten minutes wanted to know. Self-diagnosis and introspective discovery simply seemed the best therapy, at least for him.

Kyle Yoder had seen every war movie ever made. He'd thrived on them—he and his grandfather—throughout his youth. He knew *all* the clichés: he did not cringe at the sound of a car backfiring; he didn't hear voices; he didn't wake up thinking the enemy was just around some corner; he never thought he was back in Afghanistan.

He knew many men, and women, who *did* experience those things. It was the very reason so many of his Delta and other Spec Op brethren kept on fighting for other causes. Too often, it was not for the money. Such capitalization on income for skill would have actually been healthier than the truth. Many took on such jobs because it was the only option left to them that would satisfy the creatures of combat they'd become.

Or, had always been.

Yoder did find it sad that too many of his military family were returning without obvious or ample assistance, yet that sadness actually made him feel contrastingly fortunate; fortunate that he did *not* feel he needed the help that was neither available or offered.

Kyle Yoder, ex-Delta, former member, Team Spiderman, figured he'd simply lost some human quality he'd never known he had. He wasn't antisocial; it was more like agnostically so. He felt he no longer had the skills (or the desire) to interact with people on a regular basis.

He lived inside his own mind—a place he'd not known was so infinitely vast and, at times, lonely.

Yoder picked up odd jobs when he could—he learned to be a handy painter and drywall man, and often there was work available doing painting in the summer months and remodeling drywall jobs during the winter.

There were a few shelters in the city; the problem was getting off a work site early enough to make the hike across town and still find a bed available. So, Yoder had located a protected niche in a dead-end alleyway where the brutal Wyoming winds were significantly kinder and the owner of the restaurant behind which he had constructed a makeshift tent shelter did not mind him living there. The owner had served in Korea and felt strongly about veterans. Also, Yoder's continual presence there in the late hours tended to keep the riff-raff elsewhere.

So, in a strange way, his life was settling into a comfortable rhythm; nothing resembling his former existence—or any of the evolutions between high school and the war—but enough normalcy to satisfy his aching, tired mind.

Then, as if he'd stepped on a landmine, he was arrested for a crime—and not just a crime: one he did not *remember committing.*

It was difficult even for him to believe in his own innocence; after all, he'd been found, sitting there, covered in the victims' blood—four dead strangers—and Kyle with no memory of anything.

Of course, he'd said nothing to anyone about anything, much less the recent experiences of lost time. It had been happening more frequently over the previous month, but never anything as serious as the night of the murders.

A few minutes, at most, and usually when he was sleeping. He would recall lying down in his sleeping bag, inside the tent—even remember waking up at various points in the night—but sometime near dawn, the sun barely breaking the horizon far in the distance—Kyle would come fully awake and find himself inexplicably sitting in the park near the river, or on a Front Street bench, or once riding an early morning city bus (that time, clearly having had to be coherent enough to use his pass to enter the public transit).

Was it possible he had committed some terrible act when not aware of the situation? The idea was completely untenable. As a person knew when they were truly awake or dreaming, Kyle was aware enough of his reality that nothing so atrocious could have possibly happened and left him with no memory on either end of the event spectrum. It was too large a leap.

But to whom could he confide his situation? How could he seek help then, under the circumstances of being the prime suspect, and every word he uttered or action that was taken held against him?

He was a man of honor. If for whatever reason he was guilty of committing the odious crimes for which he was accused, he would not only accept responsibility, as well as whatever punishment was deemed appropriate, but would demand nothing less. Kyle Yoder would never shrink away from his own actions, right or wrong.

However, he could *not* admit to—or take responsibility for—something he *knew* in his heart he did not do.

Which meant the police would have to prove his guilt, *even to him*.

"Journalism can never be silent:
that is its greatest virtue
and its greatest fault.
It must speak, and speak immediately,
while the echoes of wonder,
the claims of triumph and
the signs of horror
are still in the air."

~Henry Anatole Grunwald

Chapter 4

THE *WYOMING Tribune Eagle's* Editor-in-Chief, Sloan Martin, knew the prominence and inevitable impact of such tragedy, particularly in a small city. Even as a news reporter, normally conversely excited inside by the calamities others dreaded—the bad things that occurred in the world; events upon which journalists had no control yet increased newsworthiness commensurately with the gravitas of the event—she could find no positivity, or even eagerness of professional duty, in such circumstances.

She cared too much for the future of Cheyenne.

Not that anyone would believe her had she told them so.

The current world seemed to think that reporters were all comparable to piranhas, or, worse, parasites, feeding off the misery of others.

Paparazzi with pens.

Most of the time, Sloan made a palpable effort to pause and remind herself that such epithets came with the job. Everything in life was a tradeoff. If a person dreamed of reporting the news, or ended up in the business by chance, it really didn't matter—the bigger the disaster, the fame (or lack thereof) about whom the story revolved, the impact of the catastrophe—the more profound and the more profitable the story.

Ergo, by twenty-first century definitions, the more newsworthy. It was not difficult to deduce the rest. Sloan Martin had chosen a profession regarded by the masses to lack empathy, decorum, or any benevolence whatsoever.

Perhaps much of the reputation bestowed over the decades was earned. The current mode of frenzied, unrestrained folly that flew across the wire at the speed of light, from every bozo's cell phone straight to the planet, wasn't helping said reputation.

But like so many other callings—law enforcement, for one—just wait until the masses *needed you.*

Doctors, too, had confided in her often; each, at some point, eventually faced with the reality that saving a precious percentage of patients also meant the inevitable loss of others. And when a family member or loved one was the receiver of crushing news, the physician soon learned the sanctuary of professional detachment. Fellowship and allowing oneself to become *involved*—to *care*—well, those, a person learned, were the privileges of other professions.

Such was the sacrifice of the journalist.

As if *that* word meant what it once did, even within the community.

Sloan was no one's fool; there were thousands—tens of thousands, even, in the new *information age*—who considered themselves journalists (in fact, who *didn't?*). Such cretins who truly *did* gorge on the un-newsworthy, caring only for leaps in a career or more money; such people had, in Sloan's mind, either deliberately, or naively, traded their integrity for the brass ring of the profession: ratings, more hits, likes, or trending.

It didn't really matter; it all equated to an adulterating of the real sickness:

Sensationalism.

Such lure to turn to the melodramatic angle on the news had always been around, tempting the reporter; since the first news story was ever recounted, it had been lurking about. Readers, listeners—they craved the theater of the everyday. It was human, albeit guilty pleasure, to desire such entertainment. But it was the duty of the journalist to filter out the information that got through—to hold back on the elements of the story to which the public at large was *not* entitled, as well as to report those facts to which they *were.* There was a fine yet steely line in protecting the privacy of the individual, *innocent* citizen.

The laws and rights laid down by the forefathers of the United States in the First Amendment guaranteed the right to report the news, but along with that right came the responsibility of assuming the accused innocent *first*, not guilty in order to garner more attention for the reporter of the story.

During the twentieth century in particular, the structure of the newsroom had been constructed with checks and balances to safeguard such ideals—section managers, proofreaders, investigators, assistant editors, editors-in-chief—there was, at least, a system through which stories were discussed on merit, assigned when approved; procedures of gathering information were followed; facts were verified by multiple, independent sources; sources vetted; copy was approved—the system wasn't foolproof, but it was a process.

Now anyone with a computer and an Internet connection—no; anyone with simply a *cell phone*—was a reporter. Everything was now on video. "Stories" happened in real time, without judge, jury, *or* executioner. Individuals filmed something, individuals watched, decided, and the story was really over before it was reported. Rarely did the term *professional* enter into the discussion.

And certainly not *journalism*.

Chief Wallace had pleaded with her when she called him, practically begging her to leave out the fact that the victims were tourists, not locals. Reminding her—unnecessarily—that such headlines and information disseminated too soon could do to the city irreparable damage.

She understood, and would have hoped because of the times they'd worked together in the past, that he would know that about her. There was a finite amount of time to put a lid on any story—regardless of how long that potentially crucial suppression would do more good than bad (and in the present case, the longer was certainly better)—and she also knew Chief Wallace was up against an untenable, situation. Still, putting up sensationalizing headlines, particularly so soon after a crime—regardless of the story—would not help the matter, nor was it the standard for an ethical news editor like Sloan.

Wallace had told Sloan in the past how much he respected her ethics and professionalism—but if he truly had, he wouldn't have needed to ask her to avoid sensationalizing the murders or to report only the pertinent facts at the time.

She was offended, not wounded. Cops and reporters had been on opposing sides so many times, superficially at war but still, fundamentally, on the same side. He still saw her as the enemy—or if not the enemy, then an antagonist; an adversarial to be controlled.

And he was a shitty cop.

Either way, Sloan required no governing (nor was she comfortable with it); such early release of anything beyond strict facts would serve no more than to incite panic amongst locals and tourists the same. If she wanted to stir up the exclusive and garner the national spotlight, she was free to report whatever she wanted.

But she'd never, in her twenty-two year career, used the First Amendment as a pretext to print—or upload—whatever story she felt would glorify her, the paper, or—early in her street reporting days, her bosses. Sloan Martin had achieved her success, and delivered the news, honorably and with journalistic professionalism. And she would do so then.

The details in such a disastrous crime would change by the hour. And the damage that would come down on the city—particularly a small town in the west; an ostensibly peaceful, recreational destination—would be profound. She may have wished Wallace had shown more faith in her integrity and intelligence, but she'd never been a self-pitying kind of woman. She felt her duty to protect Cheyenne, in any way possible, as much as Wallace.

There was no changing the gravity of such a news story. There would be no altering of the facts—neither those known or those out there, waiting to be uncovered. And both Ewan Wallace and Sloan knew the murders *had* to be reported one way or the other. Such news would dominate the headlines for a long time to come. Both of them also understood that the sensationalism of such enormous, horrific events was inherent in their sheer gruesomeness—events so abhorrent took on a persona and an ability of their own to grow and spread. Nothing Sloan reported or Chief Wallace briefed could put the brakes on the locomotive for long.

Wallace's primary responsibility would be to attempt containment of any information until the investigators could be sure that it was correct; Sloan could help him do that. She'd already informed him in their phone discussion that *the Tribune* did intend to put out an early edition of the daily newspaper, before sunrise.

Wallace had not protested.

No one read traditional newsprint anymore—no one that hadn't already seen the headline and story on a web site, or through word-of-mouth (still the quickest media in Wyoming).

Word of the village, Wallace called it—not original, but more than accurate in smaller towns and cities. Chances were good the tale was already spreading like a new fire in fresh, dry kindling wood, growing more ferocious as it consumed a forest of arid timber awaiting its arrival.

By the time the papers hit the corners and the newsstands and the front porches in the early hours, three-quarters of Cheyenne would already know the story and have formed an opinion.

Print was nothing more any longer, it seemed, than a rubber stamp of the events already in the news; a reality that saddened a seasoned reporter like Sloan Martin. But if you didn't adapt to the new world, it simply rolled over you.

The story online was up long before, but included only what was known in those first early morning hours, which wasn't much:

One witness statement and the fact that four men were dead and a local man—a war hero—had been arrested. Every murder investigation required detectives to withhold some particulars, both to manage the flow of information *and* to ensure that the police investigation stayed ahead of the public's full knowledge of the facts.

Particularly the press, Sloan knew.

But Sloan was good at her job, as was each of her staff. She'd moved to Cheyenne twelve years earlier from a job as a Managing Editor at the St. Louis Post, where she had risen quickly through the ranks with a reputation as a sound journalist.

She could get information when she wanted it, whether the police divulged it or not (another fact that annoyed her about the police chief's opinion of her abilities). Like the fact that all four murdered men were from Santa Monica, and were gay. Two couples, in fact; legally married in the state of California. Sloan had already uncovered that information with a few calls to sources in the morgue, the airport, and then to an investigator she used to work with in New York but was now in Los Angeles.

It wasn't as if *the Tribune* needed such information to keep the public informed or to satisfy their right to know. The sexual orientation of the victims was not, at present, newsworthy. It didn't pertain to the crime at that phase, so Sloan would not add anything to fuel the spectacle. She had investigated the identities and proclivities of the victims only as any sound journalist would—investigating and reporting being two very different things.

She had also wanted to prove to herself that she still had the chops.

But the newsworthiness of the men's sexual orientations was of no consequence to the first response regarding the crime.

And Cheyenne was no more a town of bigotry than anywhere else in the world—less so than many. Such information was clearly being withheld from the public to use in the investigation, and more likely the interviewing of the suspect.

Whose detailed history Sloan had also uncovered.

Sergeant Kyle Yoder, recently promoted from Corporal, a now former member of not just the United States Army, but its elite Delta Force. The identity of the accused had been released, as had part of his military service record—specifically, his decorations—but the fact that he was Delta had been withheld from the first press briefing.

And though *the Tribune* would not yet report Sloan's other investigative discovery, she knew that other "news organizations" would, once the information was uncovered and the story went viral, and Sloan was prepared with a *Tribune* story, ready for release. She needed to walk the tightrope, balancing the ethical release of early information too soon with her onus to her employer to ensure that their news organization not "get scooped" on their own story.

Earlier Sloan had called her Manager of Technology, Sri Patel, a combination IT guru, coder, and webmaster. Sri also had some less-advertised skills: writing custom application interfaces, building mobile applications, and what in the community was known as *white hat* hacking;

nothing illegal, overtly or otherwise, but a young man with the skills to find, analyze, and manipulate what information he needed online.

Sloan had not fought the online revolution. It wasn't that her heart was any less torn by the way things had changed so quickly and drastically (and not for the better) in journalism. But at the same time, one of the tenets of surviving in any business—even the *business* of delivering the news—was changing with the evolutions over time. Online news delivery had already changed the way the world expected and received their news reports.

More than she'd have liked, Sloan had relied heavily on Sri to confirm *the Tribune* was maintaining its position of leader in the reporting to the city, state, and world, online—his work for the paper and her, specifically, had been invaluable.

Sloan's cell rang. She had called her online specialist a few minutes earlier and asked him to come in. "Sri?"

"Yes, Ms. Sloan. I am leaving the house now and should be there in ten minutes."

"I'm sorry to bring you in so late, Sri."

"It's no problem, ma'am."

"I'll see you in a few minutes, then," said Sloan. "I want to talk in person."

"Understood, Ms. Sloan."

Sri disconnected and Sloan wilted into a nearby chair in the room that was, during daylight hours, the nerve center of the organization, teeming with the sound of the daily news being disseminated, crunched, edited, and fought over.

It was eerily quiet, particularly with the storm of the century gathering itself, able to burst forth and drown the small Wyoming town—and it *would* drown the city, with all the major news organizations from around the country and even the globe descending on Cheyenne.

The city was not equipped for the seriousness of the story that was about to break, and such places—particularly without the resources to control the way the pieces broke apart and were put back together—could become unwillingly *defined* by such an event.

Boston.

Oklahoma City.

Waco.

Littleton, Colorado.

Only places such as New York City could withstand such sensational events without the event defining the city itself.

Cheyenne stood little chance of not being consumed by the four murders. The only possibility of some reprieve resided with the verdict, but the chances that the young man *didn't* commit the crime, despite all the cries of innocence before guilt? Not good.

Sloan wondered at the way in which the game of life—like every other contest—was one of inches. If Yoder had still been in the military at the time of the alleged attacks, such a seemingly small matter could have sheltered the city of Cheyenne from almost all the blowback. When a soldier was tried and convicted in a court-martial, the proceeding was almost completely inaccessible to the public—the news media, in particular—and what documentation *did* eventually make it to the public was normally redacted so much it might as well be a grocery list.

Yoder was to be tried by the State, however. So not only would the city and Wyoming bear the weight of the dreadfulness, there would be a *much* longer process, with the entire proceeding, investigations, evidence, testimony, and sentencing a full matter of public record and, most likely, the media would have some kind of access to the daily happenings in one form or another.

Sloan wondered just what D.A. Forster would decide vis-à-vis the possibility of adding the charge of hate crimes against Yoder. Such an addition was negligible in the face of the greater charges, but still not inconsequential from a news-reporting point of view.

And such a pronouncement would lend the D.A. a well-honed sword in the not too distant election. Tough on crime was an expectation of the office; tough on human rights was icing for the political pastry.

Sloan would be ready for all of it: the dodge, parry, and thrust of the journalist's position. The situation would be changing by the minute, not the day or hour. The murders in Cheyenne were likely only an hour or two—maybe three—from exploding across the country, and the world— the news racing along its way by viral nature inherent in the information superhighway.

Sloan had called Chief Wallace earlier and left him a message to call her back. She wanted to reaffirm her stance that *the Tribune* would honor its duty to report only the verifiable facts, but reminded him that the clock was ticking—for all of them.

She was adamant that *The Wyoming Tribune Eagle* would not plant the inevitable seed from which international drama grew. But neither would she let some other agency garner the credit for breaking the *meat* of the story, relegating the *Tribune Eagle* to the anticipatory role of small town newspaper.

When the incident burst out, the *Tribune would* be the organization at the forefront of its reporting.

Sri Patel arrived fifteen minutes later. He met Sloan in her office.

"Sit down, please," Sloan said. "Thank you again for coming in at this hour."

"You are welcome," Sri said. "What is happening?"

"I need some technical assistance from you. Do you still maintain the app for tracking trending Internet items?"

"Stories, yes."

"Some are stories; some are not," said Sloan.

"Yes, ma'am."

"It's a nitpick of mine," she said.

"The application is healthy and running. I still use it daily."

Sri had come to Sloan two years earlier and asked for a substantial amount of money for a pair of network appliances. The devices were built by a well-known search engine company but were being marketed as more than web searchers. Web search engine appliances primarily swept the Internet, using a technology called "scraping" where they would filter terabytes of data, caching gigabytes of metadata. The appliances being requested by Sri were capable of much more than serving user searches; they ran algorithms against the data captured and reported on trending web traffic, giving any website—from rogue gossip reporting to legitimate news-reporting organizations—the ability to write stories a fraction ahead of the arrival of the events going viral.

Sri Patel wrote his own application program interface, using predictive algorithms that were capable of further filtering the data, giving the user the ability to enter search parameters that could be analyzed for potential of trending, the current and projected rate of viral spread, and was able to pinpoint when the event—based on keyword parameters—would begin trending and go viral with impressive accuracy.

Sloan leaned over her desk. "I want you to take the story I am about to email to you, use this list of keyword searches," Sloan slid a piece of paper across a small clear spot in the mountain of mess that hid her desktop, "and when it looks like the story has reached critical Internet mass, before it explodes, release the copy I will have sent you."

"When you say 'release'—" said Sri.

Sloan felt like a criminal arranging a hit; she knew the capabilities of her technical guru. He could make just about anything happen when it came to web optimization and ranking and there was nothing he could not code.

He also had a trusted list of online journalists in key organizations with more than a modicum of integrity who would gladly give the credit to the *Tribune Eagle* for a chance to be one of the first to break the story on their sites.

"*Everything* in the story I am sending you is accurate and verifiable. I won't sensationalize, but neither will the *Tribune Eagle* be trumped by either the big players or the rest of the websites wannabes. I want it clear that the first accurate reporting on the story came from the *Tribune Eagle*. Use your skills, use your sources, play your chits.

"When it's time, I want US *viral*."

Sri left with the list and said nothing more.

~

After returning to his office at midnight, still just hours after the quadruple-murder and him up thirty-eight hours straight, Chief Wallace took his cell from his inside jacket pocket. It had been blowing up for hours and he'd been ignoring it because he knew the majority of the calls were issues he did not yet want to fend—he had let them go to voicemail to begin accumulating there; a veritable pile of insurmountable work growing without his consent or involvement.

God bless the information age, he thought, weary and sarcastic beyond reason.

He grabbed a cup of coffee that had likely been on the burner since before any of the bedlam had exploded and looked like it had been scraped off the bottom of the fishpond on his grandfather's farm in western Nebraska. Adding enough sugar and cream to cover up the flavor of burned cigarettes, he sat down to listen to the critical voicemails. Wallace figured he'd take them in order, from the most recent to the oldest. This way if a newer message trumped an older one, he'd be less likely to be chasing his tail.

The newest voicemail was from Detective Wilkins, telling him they were getting nowhere with the suspect and that Yoder had invoked his right to speak to his attorney.

The next was a message from D.A. Maggie Forster, who told him the Grand Jury would be empaneled at nine A.M. and would likely take fewer than forty-five minutes to find enough evidence to indict. So the preliminary arraignment for Yoder was then set for eleven. She told Wallace she needed all information given to her as far before the nine o'clock Grand Jury proceeding as possible for her to arrange the evidence and secure the indictment.

There was a message from newspaper Editor-in-Chief, Sloan Martin, of *The Wyoming Tribune Eagle*, asking Wallace to call her back regarding new information she'd uncovered about the victims in the case.

No doubt, she knew the victims were not only tourists but married gay men from California. The lady was good at her work, but Sloan Martin knowing about the victims' proclivities worried him less than the fact that he would have to report the information to D.A. Forster, who would then probably tack on four counts of hate crimes to the suspect—not because she had any evidence of the fact, but rather as political window dressing.

The chief collapsed in his high back, expensive, calf-leather chair, closed his eyes, and ran his fingers through the tight clip of the hair left on his scalp, tiny beads of sweat already secreting from his scalp.

Normally such matters—regardless of their seriousness—would not bother him. He was, after all, supposed to be on the side of the district attorney, and any valid criminal charges against a suspect in his custody were normally no matter for concern.

But Wallace *knew* the Yoders. And he had that goddamned feeling in his gut—the one that told him if he left his own men in charge of finding the truth, Wallace the politician was going to pay for it, one way or another.

Pruett was the man he needed. James Pruett was the best cop Wallace had ever known. By a million miles. And if there was one thing Pruett hated more than anything—except maybe sobriety—was the spotlight.

Fucking guy had turned down the Army's Soldiers Medal, on principle, and then took no advantage of all the press it garnered—instead he clammed up. Wouldn't say a word.

More than that, Wallace knew Pruett loved Yoder like his own son. He'd put every ounce of his skill and mettle into proving Kyle Yoder innocent. Which also meant if the boy was guilty, Wallace was double-covered: Pruett wouldn't believe Kyle Yoder capable of such brutality, but if he discovered his godson had perpetrated those heinous murders, there was no one who would stop the man from seeing that the boy did the time for the crime.

As far as the "hate crime" potential? It was ludicrous. Wallace knew for a *fact* that Kyle Yoder was no bigot. In high school, the boy had marched on "City Hall" in a rally for gay civil rights when an amendment to the state constitution was put on the election ballot to recognize same-sex marriage in Wyoming.

In fact, the boy's record was totally clean. Not even a speeding ticket.

The boy.

Wallace had to remind himself that the Kyle Yoder in lockup was not the same boy he'd known as a child. Not only had he been to war, but he was trained Special Forces.

Still, what gave the chief—or anyone—the right to use such facts against the man? Under any other circumstance, Kyle Yoder would be honored as a *hero*. In fact, upon his return, he *was* honored as such. Cheyenne scheduled a parade for all its veterans, and Yoder was singled out as the first hometown soldier ever to receive the Medal of Honor.

The man had shaken hands with the President of the United States.

For the first time in his life, Chief Ewan Wallace did not want to be a cop; he didn't even want to be himself. He did not want to know what he knew—he wished the past hours could be erased from not only his mind but from reality.

What if Yoder did it?

What if looking good to the press meant Wallace looking on as Kyle Yoder received a lethal injection of poison?

The man put his face in his hands and wept.

The son of his friends was going to be indicted and, likely, convicted, of capital murder, and Ewan Wallace—a mediocre cop at best—might as well be the executioner.

He felt a thousand years old.

So he reached for his cell phone, tears still streaming down his face.

"...down these mean streets
a man must go
who is not himself mean,
who is neither
tarnished nor afraid.
He is the hero;
he is everything."

~Raymond Chandler

Chapter 5

KYLE YODER grew to manhood having never met his own parents. It was not a situation of abandonment or of anything other than the hand of God or of Fate or of Chance—whichever deity or lack thereof a person chose to believe. While Kyle, just over three years old, was in the care of his grandparents, his mother and father, Donna and Jeffrey Yoder, died when their 1987 pickup hit a large patch of black ice on Wyoming Highway 85/Canam Highway, north of Cheyenne, just past Lodgepole Creek. The vehicle went over into the barrow ditch sideways, flipping eight times before coming to rest on its roof.

Kyle's child seat was still buckled in the back seat, empty.

To Kyle, his parents had always been enigmatic, ephemeral notions, but at the same time very present inside his soul; spiritual consciences that were there with him, particularly at the most important moments of his life.

Raised by his grandparents, and watched over by his godfather, Kyle was never allowed to forget who his parents were—the stories, the descriptions, the pictures and videos; and Kyle felt he had known them, *physically* even, if only for such shortness of time.

Scientists and medical professionals did not theorize that the brain of a toddler before the age of five or six could form any significant, lasting memories, but Kyle *did* have them: the color of his father's blonde hair; a particular scent of perfume that immediately brought forth images of the ovular, lovely face of his mother; the brush of a soft hand along his cheek.

Most smiled along when he would share such remembrances, humoring the child, but there was never any doubt in young Kyle Yoder's mind that the images, scents, and caresses, were memories of his parents.

He definitely knew their minds and hearts; no one would ever disagree with that. His godfather—Sheriff James Pruett, across the state in Wind River, Wyoming—served in Vietnam with his father; two Wyoming boys assigned to the same platoon. Pruett may have been the man who knew Kyle's father best; a man shared things with a close friend that he might never say to a parent or other family member.

Both James Pruett and Jeffrey Yoder made it home from Vietnam—safe of body if not one hundred percent who they were before they left. Kyle had yet to be born, arriving nearly seventeen years after the war ended. Donna and Jeffrey Yoder had tried for a decade and a half to have a child, but all attempts had ended either fruitlessly or in miscarriage.

Then, just as the couple had decided they might not ever be parents, Donna got pregnant for what the two decided was the last time. *That child or none*, his father had said, and Donna had agreed. Neither of them could withstand the disappointments any longer. It had been time to move on with their lives.

And unto them, Kyle was delivered. Strong, ruddy, and healthy from the beginning. The perfect baby, his grandparents, and Sheriff Pruett told him. And after all that waiting, Kyle was, understandably, the center of his parents' worlds.

And James Pruett—six years Jeff Yoder's elder—never missed an opportunity to travel across the state and see his godson. As with everything Kyle would discover throughout his life, Sheriff James Pruett took no oath lightly. Pruett and his father had fought together, returned together, and had remained best friends.

Not only did the families get together in the summer months for fishing or the winter months for a ski trip or ice-fishing the lakes around Wind River, Kyle's godfather called on every one of the child's first few birthdays, always sent cards, presents, and even wrote the child letters for him to read when he was old enough.

And when the tragedy struck down his best friends, Pruett had stepped up even more. In fact, Kyle Yoder's first definitive memories were of phone calls, every Saturday evening—sometimes from the Sublette County Sheriff's station, his godfather on duty; other times from home, where Kyle would also talk to Aunt Bethy, as he called her.

Kyle's grandfather made a fine surrogate father for him throughout his youth, but surrogates and replacements were not the same thing. Not that his grandfather, Alton, had ever lay claim to such; in fact, he'd always made it a point to teach Kyle the difference.

Alton had encouraged the relationship that developed over the years between Pruett and Kyle, telling the boy it was crucial; that such a bond might indeed be the closest Kyle would ever have to one with his true father.

So the boy in Cheyenne and the sheriff from Wind River had become pen-pals, too, writing letters every week—unless, of course, one or the other came to visit; Kyle had spent several summers with the Pruetts (and had developed a pretty strong crush on the older Wendy, despite her standoffishness then).

Kyle was always grateful to his grandfather for allowing him to connect with Sheriff Pruett. His grandfather had been right: their relationship offered the boy an opportunity, as he grew to manhood, to learn all about the man his father had been.

"You will never have a father," Pruett had told him in one letter. "Not in this lifetime, Kyle. But when it matters; when it counts—I've seen his tenacious, decent spirit in *you*. I cannot fill the hole inside a young man that was carved for his true father, but I'll always be there for you. Best of times; worst of times. That's how it is with family, son. I want you to know that because too many young men grow up forever empty in that place. I share everything with you so that, whenever you have to decide in life what it is that you must do, or choose, you'll have that reservoir of knowledge—or at least as much as I can give you—and you'll know everything I knew about the man your father was."

Being from a family steeped in military tradition of service, and the innate desire to carry on that history, is why the most mentally and physically talented of all the Yoder men dreamed of being 1st Special Forces Operational Detachment-Delta.

Not a SEAL, or Airborne, or a Ranger—Delta Force.

Yoder had never seen the point in concerning himself with which Spec Op military organization was the finest; in his mind, they were all equally fierce, and represented the most elite of the fighting patriots. But since he could remember—maybe because his father had revered them so; perhaps only chance—Kyle Yoder wanted nothing less than to achieve the ranks of Delta.

And it wasn't as if the boy had no options. He'd made the 2009 *Under Armour All American Football Team*; no small honor, particularly from a player in the state of Wyoming, where "few recruiters roamed," Yoder's coach liked to say.

The top desk drawer in the boy's bedroom was full of athletic letters— letters of interest; letters inviting him to visit campuses; and even full-blown offer letters. Recruiters and coaches had visited his home more times than he could count. Big football schools. Good schools:

Auburn. Stanford. Texas A&M. Nebraska. Iowa. Michigan. Notre Dame.

And of course, there were all the schools from both the Western Athletic and the Mountain West Conferences. Teams like TCU, Wyoming, Brigham Young, Utah, Colorado State, Hawai'i, and many more.

His grades and entrance exam scores would also have gotten him into any school he wanted to attend; the academic letters and offers of grants and fellowships and scholarships filled the *second* drawer in his desk.

Yet the very morning after the Kelly Walsh High School graduation ceremony, and the handing to him of his diploma, Kyle Yoder was waiting at the Army recruitment office, downtown Cheyenne, at 6:00 A.M.—before the duty sergeant had even arrived to open the doors.

Yoder's grandparents had not understood his desire to turn away from *so many* excellent opportunities so quickly and, seemingly, without thought or measurement. By then his grandfather seemed to have forgotten what his own patriotism felt like; his choice had been to serve in World War II. Kyle knew he'd never sway his grandmother—she had never wanted her own husband to put himself in harm's way—she was understandably mortified to think of the same for her beloved, innocent grandson.

Kyle appreciated their feelings on the matter. Such a decision did seem a bit delusional when considering the enormity of the prospects for Kyle's future that had been laid at his feet. It made sense that his grandparents would only want what was best for their grandson. In fact, he had already determined what their first rebuttals would be:

"Why not the Naval Academy, then?" his grandfather had persisted. "They have a football team, and a damn fine Special Forces unit, if that's really where you find yourself wanting to serve in the future."

And they did have all that. From a purely logistical standpoint, the Naval Academy, and the service that followed, would not only allow him to be a patriot for his country but also offered yet another of the armed forces most elite and challenging Special Forces combat training divisions in existence.

But such a choice meant even more years of waiting until he could *serve*.

This was, of course, what his grandfather was counting on.

A change of heart.

What guardian would *not* wish for their child to stay forever out of harm's way—and offer enough time for a mind to change—especially with so many other options?

Yet Kyle knew his father would have understood—he'd learned enough from Sheriff Pruett for that to be a surety. And even though Kyle knew it caused the sheriff mixed feelings, ultimately Pruett supported what he knew to be his godson's greatest desire.

Over the years—through the letters, and the private conversations out in a boat, in the center of majestic tranquility, closer, perhaps, to his father's spiritual presence than anywhere else in the world—Pruett had realized that there was little to no chance of changing Kyle's determination.

So, beginning the boy's sophomore year in high school, Pruett had insisted that if Kyle was not to be swayed from his patriotic duty, and if his goal was definitely Delta Force, there wasn't going to be any half-assed assault on the dream.

Pruett schooled Kyle on the realities of politics and placements and the physical demands expected of him that would make three-a-days in football seem like yoga classes.

Unknown to his grandfather, Pruett had insisted Kyle completely change his training regimen. Kyle spent extra hours in the off-season, and even after practices, climbing all over the most rugged terrain he could find, with a backpack filled with weights—most of the incline work being done to the west, in the forest and mountains between Cheyenne and Laramie, at high altitude.

"It won't be enough to have the cardiovascular endurance of a high school—or even college—football player," Pruett had told him. "Delta will require you to exert yourself in places and directions and over longer periods of time than a human being is designed to withstand. That's half the point. They will be weeding out soldiers who have spent their careers kicking ass on anything that moves; winning every challenge put in front of them. Some of the most conditioned men you will ever meet will plead to be allowed the *privilege* of ringing out the first day."

Pruett also explained to him the importance of his early assignments, particularly in the early phases of his enlistment.

"One of the most crucial decisions that get made could very well be where you go for Basic," Pruett told him. "You need to be as well educated as the recruitment sergeant—heck, probably *more so*—about where you want to be assigned first. Request OSUT—that's short for *One Station Unit Training*. It combines Basic and Advanced Individual Training. Jump school at Benning is another must.

"You need to understand something, Kyle," Pruett had said. "Most of the men who will train for Delta are recruited, just like football or anything else. And the recruitment comes from the Berets and the Rangers. So the sooner you get to Fort Benning, get your jump wings, and get on the Special Forces track, the better your chances will be. Know this going in: you have a minimum of four years and E-4 grade, so there's time—but many a Delta wannabe has missed the window of opportunity because they weren't prepared beforehand. Tell your recruiter, your drill sergeant, your first commanding officer—hell, son, you tell anyone who will listen to you that you want Delta.

"Yeah, you'll catch your share of shit. But you're going to catch your fair share anyway. Making Delta is *not* for introverted soldiers; Delta is for the out of the gate gung ho."

Kyle's father won both an Army Silver Star and a Purple Heart for his service in Vietnam. The boy had never asked Pruett why he turned down the Soldiers Medal. By then his own father had been buried with his medals and Kyle knew Sheriff Pruett withstood a nation's scrutiny—as well as that of the state and his own town. Yoder figured he knew the man well enough that whatever choice he'd made, he did out of a deep love and honor for his country, and no other reason than that.

And Kyle had hoped, deep inside that his grandfather, too, understood. Even though for the men of his father and grandfather's times, the military had been one of the only options, those men still made their decisions proudly and without hesitation. How could his grandfather not understand his deep desire to serve his country?

Dutifully; bravely; patriotically.

And willingly.

Kyle Yoder had reminded his grandfather, Alton, that the elder Yoder, too, had *enlisted.* Yes, the reasons, and the threat were different—the aggression of the enemy more overtly naked and set on global dominion—but the dangers in 2010 and 2011, were serious in their own right, and terrorism threatened freedom in a global sense, as well. Al Qaeda and the Taliban had proven in 2001 they were willing to bring their barbarism and death to innocent, free people, even on United States' soil.

Kyle Yoder—a third generation of family men serving their country—wanted to be at the front line of the war against any faction intent on terrorizing innocents.

Emal Khan Ahmadzai grew to manhood halfway around the world but with no less resolve than Kyle Yoder in Cheyenne, Wyoming. Still, he would not have rationalized the same choices. There was no drawer full of letters offering opportunities—or even options—to the young Pakistani. The boy had spent most of his pre-teen years moving around, crisscrossing the border of Pakistan and Afghanistan, living for short periods of time with one manner of relative or another; at times he would be taken in by a Pashtun tribesman who, because of the boy's heritage, felt historical obligation.

Since the NATO insurgency after 9/11 in 2001, the regions where Emal Khan found himself looking for a home were commonly decimated, bereft of even the simplest supplies such as flour or even clean drinking water. It was this lack of life-sustaining necessities that kept Emal Khan on the move; no family, regardless of love, altruism, or duty could afford to put the boy's needs above those of their *own* children and immediate family (who were already wasting away into skeleton caricatures of who they'd once been).

Eventually it was the Taliban who offered Emal Khan Ahmadzai food, water, shelter, and a cause in which to place the patriotism not so unlike that of Americans like Kyle Yoder; a cause that he not only came to support, but to devour as the wild pig devours the defenseless goat. Emal Khan was starving for the satiation of a cause in which to believe; an inclusion in a brotherhood that would save his country, their religion, and a way of life that had existed for thousands of years.

At the finish of most battle days, Emal Khan and small groups of scattered Taliban forces, would hide away in deep mountain fortresses, made just for them, elegantly, Emal Khan believed, by the great Allah. Turning granite to home; sparing those who survived the day so that they might have further opportunity to serve the cause against the infidel. In Emal Khan's mind, Allah provided them with strategic niches—seemingly insignificant slices from the terrain—for the righteous to live in Spartan comfort so that the honor of bringing down *Jihad* on their enemies would be theirs, and their first reward would be to witness victory.

Each night after final prayer, before exhaustion overcame him, Emal Khan Ahmadzai promised himself that not only would he and his mujahideen brothers *win*, but that the name of *Emal Khan Ahmadzai* would travel the world, nestling itself into the very black heart of America, in Washington, from where the infidels spied on his people, built their insignificant war machine, and launched themselves halfway around the world to wage a war on an innocent, believing people.

His own prophecy of infamy, although always secondary to the cause, would indeed become reality.

2014, at an undisclosed Air Force Base, Stateside

By then Kyle was just "Yode" to everyone—all but to his second surrogate father, Sheriff Pruett, and the rest of his immediate family, who would always call him by his birth name.

Also by then Yode was a proud member of that elite group of which he'd always dreamed—Delta Force—the Army's unit dedicated singularly to the defeat of terrorism, wherever it meant they needed to be.

This would be Yode's fourth battle deployment, though first as a member of Delta Force. Sheriff Pruett had told Kyle years earlier that it was not possible to fully prepare for one's reaction to the stench of battle exploding all around him the first time, and that advice, as well as the letter given him that same day, had been enough added mental equilibrium to probably have saved the young soldier's life then.

That first deployment overseas had been as a Ranger, and Yode's first operational assignment had turned into a firefight that was over in fewer than twenty minutes, but with a sixty percent casualty loss for the NATO forces. Outnumbered and ambushed, it was the cocksure advice of his godfather that had kept Specialist Yoder calm that day.

Since then, and what Kyle had never told Pruett, was that the young man had carried the letter with him as a talisman, safeguarded it, ever since that milestone day where he could have been dead before he ever fought another battle.

Even then, in 2014, as he prepared to leave for Afghanistan, the paper was folded carefully and slipped into a plastic map protector—tucked in his utilities, wrinkled and faded from all the times it had been opened, reread, or just held in his hand.

"You'll be missed, as usual," said Pruett, stoic as ever.

"Don't get weepy on me," said Kyle.

"Boy, don't make me pin your ears back. You may be Delta, but I have a few moves left in me."

"I'll take your word for it."

"Says the man who tears up when he watches that god-awful chick flick, *The Notebook*," Pruett said.

"I'm comfortable enough with my masculinity to venture into unmanly genres," Kyle said. "And you sure as shit welled up a few times during *Saving Private Ryan*," said Kyle.

"Watch your language, *Yode*," Pruett growled. "That's a man's movie, besides."

"Yes, *sir*."

Pruett glanced over at him, grinning.

The dance of the male species; so different from most women in such moments, that unspoken male discomfort at not knowing how to say what each wanted.

Kyle's unit was boarding a plane bound for Manas air base outside Biskek, Kyrgyzstan. The logistics of sending troops to Afghanistan had been one of the toughest puzzles to solve throughout the war. Most supplies went by freighter ship, and could take weeks to be reunited with their units.

Delta brought all their necessary gear. Just as classified materials were given special treatment—shipped by air rather than sea—so, too, were the military's Special Forces and their equipment. Kyle's unit of twenty-five was traveling with seventy paratroopers from various divisions. Over seven hundred soldiers total, with all cargo—men, women, and supplies—heading in various directions from Manas.

The behemoth C-17 was also being loaded with palletized freight—food, clothing, water, munitions, and other basic supplies for the troops on the ground. Those supplies were needed in dozens of forward operating bases, or FOBs, and since the late 2000s had become harder and harder to deliver, based on the Taliban's increased control of a circular supply route known as "the ring road."

The Delta team had been fully briefed on their destination and mission, which had nothing to do with moving supplies. They were deploying as support to the 4th Brigade Combat Team—BCT—82nd Airborne Division, in an attempt to insert behind the Taliban's tribal armies' sporadic lines. Highly reliable intel—both satellite reconnaissance and human intelligence from an asset high in the Taliban regime—had given the CIA a proximate location of one of the most high-valued NATO targets.

But Kyle could tell his godfather none of it. Everything was classified. How he wanted to; wanted more than anything to share with the man he considered his best friend in the world—considered his *father*—the importance of what he was leaving to do.

As if he'd read young Kyle's mind, Pruett said, "I know you're all twisted up inside, son. And I know if you all are deploying somewhere, you're about to make me and this country very proud. We're lucky to have men like you."

"I'm so glad you could make it," Kyle said, and put his arm around Pruett's considerable shoulder. "It means more than I can say."

Pruett put his arm over the top of his godson's. "I wouldn't miss it. And you know the family would have come up if they were well enough, Sergeant," Pruett said.

Corporal Kyle Yoder had attained the rank of E5/Sergeant just the week before this fourth deployment to Afghanistan. He hadn't even told Pruett yet, but there was no point in being surprised.

"My folks—grandparents—they're getting old, Sheriff. You'll check in on them?"

"As always," said Pruett, half-smiling. "We're all getting old. Never thought this day would get here."

"I told you I'd make it," Kyle said.

"Never doubted that part for a second," Pruett said. "Wasn't sure you'd get there as fast as the Army would allow it by regulation, though. Guess I should've known."

"Never hurt that you taught me the fast track."

"No."

"Or the calls you probably made to a colonel or two."

"I may have put some shine on the car, Kyle. You drove her to the finish line."

"I still want you to know I wouldn't be here if it weren't for you," Kyle said, holding back the sadness they were both feeling—an empty place where, if life was fair, Jeffrey Yoder would be standing there with them.

His first deployment as Delta.

"Proud of you, Sergeant," said Pruett.

The two men hugged just as an airman called for the D-boys to muster their gear and head for the plane.

"I'll do you proud, Sheriff."

The two shook hands and hugged once more—quick, manlike.

Once on the plane, Yode chose a private seat, leaving a few empties between him and Trig Bowen. Most of the Delta men had their own rituals for everything, from preflight to pre-engagement.

Yode stowed his duffle, rifle, helmet, and personal backpack, securing them with carabineers and the plane's provided hooks. After they were airborne, he took the envelope from inside his utility jacket, removed the paper from the map holder, and began reading the worn, wrinkled letter:

Kyle,

This is a difficult letter to write. No more than now have I wished to still have your father by both our sides. I can tell you he would have been beyond proud, son.

And that's something I've never told you, either, but presumed you understood:

I want to make it clear now—I don't call you 'son' because your father is not here. That would imply duty. I call you that because I consider you as such. Not by blood, and I never pretended that I could replace Jeff—my friend; your real father. But I've tried over the years to help instill in you what I knew most about him—about who he was at his core—and what I believed he would have tried to instill in you.

A man going to war is no small thing, regardless of the objective, the hours spent training, learning skills, putting them to use—there is no training field that equals that of true battle. Your trainers and leaders can only do so much to prepare you.

The stench of battle is like no other in a man's lifetime. It <u>will</u> shock you. Let it. But it will begin to surprise you to feel as if you recognize it. And that will happen, too. Many of the sights and sounds and things you will see, despite your training, will overwhelm you—some so overpowering they will try to forcibly insert themselves and their awfulness down into your soul, Kyle.

Some will succeed; some things you see will scar you. And that is no failure on your part. In fact, it means there is a piece of you that is human, and you can never release your hold on that part of you. The horror that does make its way into your being must never be allowed to hold that ground, soldier. You can never let war dictate who you are.

That being said, you are charged with an awful, immensely important duty, and whatever or however the thing we call 'war' meets you, it will at first want to terrify you. That is where your training will carry you past. But the fear and the rush can be good; allow them to fuel you; reenergize you when it feels like your body and will are spent. Don't feel ashamed to embrace the innate need inside to succumb to the contradictory pleasure of battle—even of killing. War is <u>not</u> civilization; rather the human race attempting to reshape it.

But at some point, you will feel like it is some kind of elixir from the gods. It may seem as if you are joining with it—as if it is becoming a part of you. It is. In fact, it's already inside you, from long before you were dreaming of Delta.

The industrial sights and sounds and smells: cordite and explosives detonated; the metallic clank and aroma of myriad spent artillery brass; the human equivalents, each with its own distinctive smell or sound: sweat, panic, heroism, flesh—living, dying, and dead—death, and fear; earthly sights and smells: dirt and shattered concrete and sand and trees and mud and stone; and then, always, the draw of first blood, newly released to the atmosphere of this world, with an odor not unlike sweetened metal—honey and brass, your father called it.

Honey and brass.

There will be a hundred other smells. Maybe a thousand—but the visceral existence of war, it is recognizable to any man or woman, giving them a primal déjà vu in their core.

You can think of it this way: it is the unrecognized, unwritten smell of our world. Your father and I talked about this for hours, Kyle, using each other's backs to keep off the soaked ground as the rain came down upon us, 'drowning us without cleansing a single one of our sins', your father would say. What we figured out in those deluges, those seemingly endless days and nights being pounded down by nature herself, I share with you now in the hopes it helps wherever you are headed.

Remember this, if nothing else: there are no first battles. We've always been a people of war—not just Americans or Vietnamese or Afghans or Romans or any other nationality or creed. The human race is, your father and I realized, finally, its own enemy.

Our world has been put together, piece-by-piece, border-by-border, continent-by-continent, through the hellish machinations of war. There isn't an empire or a line on earth that wasn't forged in those awful furnaces. It's been that way since the beginning of time and it will be the manner in which all of it'll end one day.

But that should allow you to be at peace with your mission; it's no different a mission than those of millions of soldiers before you, over thousands of years, and thousands of battles.

It's coded in our DNA. And that is why the sights and sounds and even what we feel about it deep in our core, seem oddly familiar. And yes, we detest it—both the familiarity and the insanity of it all. But to <u>survive</u>—and make no mistake, Kyle, I write this to you that you DO and WILL survive this thing—son, you must also learn to love war a little. That's what I was trying to say before. And so it's the loving of it, only as much as it takes you, individually, that gets you through the worst of it. And when binding with it makes you feel barbaric, unkind, or even inhuman, know that it is by war's own humanity, you can hold on to the human in yourself.

For though many of the enemy are not unlike you—men or women or even children, carrying out orders—do not forget for a moment that they will take you down and steal everything you've come to consider so dear. Not because they are inherently evil, necessarily, but because they fight for what they cherish most, too. Their orders are the same as yours: to kill every one of you and your teammates.

Evil will always exist. In the form of naked territorial aggression or now, in the form of twisting religion in the name of terror. But because evil will always exist, in one or more of its forms, and because it will always seek domination over good—contrary to what the poets and artists and those who pray for peace would tell us—war <u>is</u> necessary.

And its mechanism is us.

"Remember that man
lives only in the present,
in this fleeting instant;
all the rest of his life is
either past and gone,
or not yet revealed."

~Marcus Aurelius

Chapter 6

Wednesday, July 22ⁿᵈ, 2015
11:57 P.M.

PRUETT SAT in his new office chair, having negotiated the real estate deal with Tegeler Anderson. The freshly grooved and painted sign hanging outside the small two-room, remodeled office said "Pruett Investigations."

Tegeler had given the ex-sheriff a better-than-good deal on the place. Anderson Realty easily did three-quarters of the buying, selling, renting, and otherwise of land in Wind River. The realty also had an office in Big Tree that was going on ten years old plus two brand new ventures in Jackson.

When Pruett came to Anderson and told him of his intentions, Anderson had offered him the office space on the spot and didn't want any lease or contract from the ex-sheriff. He told Pruett that as sheriff he'd served the county and townships long enough—ten times over—and that he deserved a place right there, where he could look at the County building.

Although he'd never been on the side of a negotiation where he was offering more than the deal on the table, Pruett insisted that later, after he'd settled and had a few clientele, they would sign a proper lease arrangement. Tegeler Anderson told him they'd cross that bridge when there was a bridge to cross.

Pruett spent the next few weeks cleaning, repainting, and making the place his own. He purchased some reasonable office furniture in Idaho

Falls. He hung a few pictures—one Mangelsen: a gorgeous polar bear with her three cubs; the mother clearly enjoying the moment as much as the young ones. That particular piece of photography art had always been Bethy's favorite, so keeping that one close to him at his new digs helped the old man feel more at home.

Pruett's own favorite Mangelsen was still at the cabin: a magnificent tiger, in a hunting pose, unsuspecting prey somewhere outside the zoom of the camera's lens, the tiger's every muscle engaged, prepared, ready to lunge. That piece represented the animal within him, dissatisfied with the new town structure, regardless of what he attempted to maintain on the outside. He'd thought of bringing that one, too, but knew to look at it every day would only intensify the feeling that he was lost. Pruett; the predator who knew not what would be *his* next meal.

It wasn't as if there was a lot of P.I. work in Wind River (although, he reminded himself, Tom Selleck had always seemed to do all right on the relatively secluded island of Oahu). The new business was, in the early stages, for personal reconnaissance. Whatever needs the town housewives had in discovering their cheating husbands or the latest trend of building family trees and finding lost relatives on the Internet, well, Pruett figured he could handle that, too.

Until Pruett could accept retirement—until he could accept that he was no longer the law in Wind River—he'd have to know his town was in good hands. Convincing his old staff to remain on duty and not leave in silent protest had been a big step in that direction. Of course Pruett had worried that the inexperienced Jake Walker would not realize the good fortune inherent in their staying, but he had at least recognized the benefit in keeping the two deputies, their loyalties notwithstanding.

Baptiste was the best cop Pruett knew—small town or otherwise—and Melody Munney had come a long way in her years under Sheriff Pruett. With them backing up the sheriff work of Walker, Pruett could at least manage a few hours of sleep each night.

Zach Canter had pulled Pruett aside before he returned to Cody and offered to move back and apply for any position that eventually became available. Canter was good stock, and Pruett had thanked him with honest gratitude for his loyalty, but in the end, he wanted happiness for his deputies, too, and Pruett politely told him to return to his new home and enjoy family and life.

So there old man Pruett was, a private investigator without anything to officially investigate—sitting in his office nearing midnight. He had to admit that part of the reason for the office was so that he had somewhere else to be, that wasn't home, but that also wasn't a bar.

Pruett was trying on his "thinking cap" at the new office, hoping it would serve him as a place where he could come and feel like a *cop*. That he had no work, yet—well, that was beside the point, in Pruett's mind.

Additionally, such a lull would serve him for the current situation. From where he chose to arrange his desk and chair, he could look easily and see the second floor ledge across the street that was his sheriff office for nearly three decades.

Holding the illusion of his own acceptance of the situation was not going to be easy; so Pruett had sworn to not shrink from the change but, rather, keep it at bay, in his face, never to forget his ultimate charge—one that was not created nor destroyed by any vote.

It also kept Sheriff Walker under his watch.

Just because Pruett no longer wore the badge didn't mean he didn't carry the experience, and his experience told him there was something not right about the campaign and election of Jake Walker. Aside from other poor character traits, Walker was a politician at his core, not a lawman.

Pruett's cell phone rang, ripping him from thought and as he answered it, he wondered if sole proprietors even needed office phones any longer, because that was one thing he'd forgotten to buy.

"Pruett."

"James Pruett. It's good to hear your voice."

"Wallace?"

"Damn straight," said Chief Wallace. "I was sorry to get word of the election over there in Wind River but I never could muster the will to call you about it."

"Old friends don't need to call every time a man's knee gets scraped."

"A bit more than that, Jimmy."

"It is what I allow it to be," said Pruett.

"Fair enough," Wallace said. "I called primarily about a different matter."

"Go on, Ewan. Happens I've got some time on my hands."

"You sittin'?"

"As it happens, I am. What's happened?"

"Thing like this, it's difficult to put a price tag on it, Jimmy. Hard to find the words to explain the situation. You know the drill."

"Who's died," asked Pruett. It was the obvious question and he was on the other side of the conversation now and didn't want to make Ewan Wallace find the words that were the most impossible to locate.

"Afraid it's more complicated than that," said Wallace. "A lot more complicated."

"I'll do all I can to help you, Ewan. But you're holding all the cards. What the hell has happened?"

"Kyle Yoder is being arraigned for murder in the first," Wallace said as evenly as he could. "Four counts."

"Murder?" Pruett's body felt weightless, as if he might float out of his chair. Reality was a long way from setting in; he needed to hear the words again. This time he was more deliberate—he tried to put on the hat of a lawman. "Kyle Yoder—my godson; a perfect student; war hero; nicest guy anyone might want to meet—you're calling to inform me that my boy, Kyle, has gone and killed, what, four people?"

"Jimmy, there ain't an easy way to put this. You know that. But I have to—"

"I'm hanging up now," said Pruett. "I'll call you back, Ewan. It's better for us both. I need to think for a minute. Thanks for calling me; thank you for being the one."

The phone slipped from Pruett's grasp and fell to the floor before his friend in Cheyenne could answer one way or the other. Pruett felt as though he was sliding down a well, his arms and legs spread, trying desperately to slow the fall.

In an attempt to return to reality, Pruett tried to think of the situation as would any cop. Terrible things happened every day and officers of the law—all first responders—saw the worst of it. Wallace said it himself: there was no way to put something as egregious as what must have happened out east into words, and not over the phone.

The earth still felt removed from beneath the big man, and his descent down the well hastened. His heart felt swollen and ineffectual; though it was beating, over two hundred clicks a minute. Soon darkness began to crawl in from the fringes of his vision, the well into which he was falling expanding into an infinite cave of obsidian darkness and, just as the world dissolved altogether, James Pruett whispered his wife's name and fell to the floor, next to his phone.

Thursday, July 23rd, 2015
12:42 A.M.

When he finally regained consciousness in the Wind River Medical Clinic, the light about him did not seem heavenly or as if he was witnessing angels. It was simply ugly, yellow bulbs and that nauseating, antiseptic smell of the hospital.

Mercifully, although he knew who he was and, to an extent, where he was, Pruett did not remember his collapse or—yet—the phone call he had received before it.

"You're awake," said Doc sawbones, Jeb Percy.

"Always knew you were a fine doctor," Pruett said, as if sedated. "Now I know it to be true."

"Take it easy," said Dr. Percy. "Too much of that James Pruett salt and vinegar isn't good for a man who just survived his first heart attack."

"Heart attack?" said Pruett.

"A fairly mild one, we think. Anything more severe, we'd have flown you up to Jackson or down to Salt Lake. Count yourself lucky you're waking up to my ugly mug."

"Was in my new office," said Pruett, more to himself than to Percy.

"Something set you off?" said the doc.

"I got a phone call. Some bad news—the kind most people don't deal with well."

His memory was back like an angry migraine. And it *did* hurt his head—more because of how little he knew than how much. He started to sit up, but before Doc Percy could protest, Pruett's own body slammed him back onto the slightly elevated hospital bed.

"Ugh," Pruett exhaled, tendrils of pain spreading outward from his chest toward all parts of his body.

"You need to stay one hundred percent immobile until we know more about your condition, James."

"How long was I down?" said Pruett, face still twisted in a grimace of anguish.

"You've only been out, oh, less than an hour."

"Shit," Pruett managed. "Get me my cell phone."

"Can't," said Percy. "You're too weak. And I won't let you reconnect with whatever might have started this."

Pruett would have fought him but he'd never felt so powerless or in as much pain. Not since his squad found him after a brief skirmish with the Vietcong, Pruett sprayed with shrapnel from a mine that exploded over twenty yards away. The pain then had been excruciating and he'd believed he would die there in the leaves and undergrowth of Vietnam.

"Do me a favor then," he whispered.

"If I can."

"Call Red Horse Baptiste."

"He's in the waiting area; with half the damn town. Including Sheriff Walker."

"Then go get him."

"No one can be in here now, James. I'm not kidding around. You're not out of danger just yet. At least we can't be certain."

Pruett opened his eyes and locked them with his doctor and friend. "Get. Him."

12:58 A.M.

Baptiste took what his old boss told him to "Pruett Investigations" and opened the door with the key Pruett gave him. He turned on the lamp, picked up the ex-sheriff's cell, and dialed the last incoming number.

"Pruett?" the voice on the other end answered. "What happened? Are you okay—?"

"This is Sublette County Deputy Red Horse Baptiste."

"Uh, okay. Where is James Pruett?"

"He is in the hospital. He's expected to recover, but he is weak now. Can't talk; doc won't let him. You need to talk to me so that I can get word to him and assist."

"He always spoke fondly of you," said Wallace.

"What happened?" Baptiste said, sticking to the point.

Chief Ewan Wallace explained what had been discovered the night of the murders—and what had transpired since. "The Laramie County D.A. and I have a good working relationship. If she knew I was calling you now she would have my balls in a sling, Deputy. You know how this all works; we're on the side of the law and of justice."

"Sometimes the line blurs in these matters," said Baptiste. "There are times even lawmen must make a stand."

"That may be true. And James Pruett may have the luxury of knowing Kyle Yoder could never have committed this terrible crime. Hell, *I'm* not anywhere near sure on this thing. But I am the Chief of Police and there are four dead bodies in my city morgue. Four murders. And the only one at the scene of the crime—the only man *capable* of killing four men—is Kyle Yoder. What am I supposed to do with that?"

"What you are now."

"What I am now," said Wallace. "Aiding the defense, is what they call *what I'm doing now.*"

"You're a cop. Like me. Over the years, we learn to trust our instincts. That's all I see here: a cop reaching out to another cop and sharing his gut reaction."

"That and a pile of inside information," said Wallace.

Baptiste brought the conversation back to the facts. "What will the charges be?"

"D.A. Forster is going to ask the Grand Jury in the morning to indict Yoder with four counts of capital murder. His training mandates charges of first-degree murder whatever his intent or lack thereof. He is considered a lethal weapon."

"What happened there last night, Chief?"

"That's what I need to find out."

"Do you trust this district attorney?"

"I told you we have worked well together. I'm not sure I know her well enough to answer that question. She's never given me reason to *distrust* her."

"Then we start from there. As you said: stick to the facts. Let the law and the evidence lead us to where we need to be."

"My fear is that there won't be any way for me to authorize further investigations beyond the point of the State feeling it has a case. My duty is to assist the prosecutor in getting a conviction."

"Not of an innocent man, it's not."

"No," Wallace agreed. "But gut feeling for the son of a friend isn't going to be enough to warrant investigating against the grain."

"Which is why we're talking now, correct, Chief?"

"That is why we are talking now, Deputy. And also why we won't be able to talk like this much again."

"Then give me what we need to know. The defense is entitled to have all the evidence heard. We'll find the evidence."

"This is way off the books, Deputy."

"What else?" said Baptiste, writing notes on a pad.

"My detectives uncovered the name of a potential second witness. She cut out of her shift early and the patrol car sent to her house found nothing. Empty. Her name is Allison Chapman."

"What else?"

"The lab came back with the results of the blood examination from the crime scene. There were five matches with the victims and the suspect. But there were trace amounts of a sixth sample that did not match any of the five."

"Prints, DNA, a weapon?"

"No weapon. The DNA results are still not back."

"How can we contact you?" said Red Horse.

"Carefully," said Wallace. "Give me your number, not Pruett's. I think it's better if you and I talk. Pruett is too much of a known entity."

"I need to get this information to the sheriff."

"He's not Sheriff Pruett anymore, Red Horse. You need to keep him mindful of that fact. Even if he were, he'd have no jurisdiction here. He starts pushing his muscle around here in Cheyenne, I'll be forced to do what I'm paid to do. I won't want to. So when I say *off the books*, this thing is out of the ballpark, okay?"

"He won't be alone on this," said Baptiste.

"I know he won't."

1:24 A.M.

After a briefing of the known facts from Baptiste, Pruett told the deputy to call Wendy, explain the situation—emphasizing that her father was OKAY—and then to fill her in on what little he knew about the Kyle Yoder situation in Cheyenne.

Wendy and her fiancé, law professor and defense attorney, J.W. Hanson, lived in Laramie, Wyoming, which was only a short one-hour drive from Cheyenne.

"I need to speak with Jay as soon as possible," Pruett said. "Doc Percy isn't going to like it but you try and figure something out."

A few minutes later, Baptiste came back in, looking like the dog who had shit the rug and been caught. Apparently, Doc Percy wasn't happy to discover Red Horse running errands for the patient.

"I spoke to Wendy," said Baptiste. "She took some calming down."

"And?"

"She wasn't too keen on talking about the situation in Cheyenne at first, I can tell you that. When she wants to be, that girl can rival a bobcat protecting her kittens."

Pruett was uneasy. "I ain't feeling so hot here, Red Horse. I know you're fond of Wendy. Were you able to talk to her about Jay or not?"

"Yep. I told her you were going to be fine. When she riled down, I asked her if she knew what had happened with Yoder. She said the professor and her, they just got back from Fort Collins. So I filled her in."

"And?"

"She couldn't believe it. First thing out of her mouth was to ask if that's what put you down."

"Shit," said Pruett. "What about Hanson?"

Baptiste produced a cell phone he'd gotten past the questionable defenses of Percy and his two nurses. "He's calling here in five minutes."

"You go out and occupy Percy," Pruett said. "Keep him out of here for me."

"I'll try, boss."

A few minutes later, the cell rang.

"Jay?"

"James. Are you all right?"

"I'm going to be right as rain," Pruett said. "How much have you uncovered on the Yoder situation in Cheyenne?"

"I've read what's out there, which isn't a lot. They'll have no recourse in a case like this but to ask that he be indicted with capital crimes, James."

"How is that possible?" Pruett said. "I mean, the facts of the case, according to Chief Wallace suggest a high possibility of self-defense."

Hanson was silent for a beat. "There are four men dead, James. It's not going to do us any good talking speculation; you know that better than anyone."

"Wallace said something about an inept public defender."

"I already called the district attorney. She and I have known each other for quite a while. It's a love hate relationship. But I already filed a motion with the court clerk to instate me as the defense attorney of record. I'll be there for the preliminary arraignment."

"Will he get bail?" Pruett said.

"I'll ask for it," said Hanson. "But it will be denied. There's an automatic remand for capital crimes in Wyoming. The final decision is still left with the judge, who can hear cases of extreme circumstance, but I've never seen a suspect charged with a capital offense be granted bail."

"So he rots in jail while the trial drags on?"

"The proceeding shouldn't take a long time. The court system here isn't as clogged as bigger districts in New York or California. The docket here should be manageable."

Pruett cut him off. "How long for the trial?"

"With the current evidence, motions, testimony of experts—"

"What *experts*?"

"Psychiatric experts," Hanson said.

"An insanity defense?"

"James, I know it sounds bad, but in Kyle's circumstances, with no other theories or suspects, and the only witness being for the prosecution—one who will testify under oath that he found Kyle there, within a few feet of all four dead bodies, their blood all over him—"

Hanson stopped. He realized Pruett wouldn't have had time to process the prosecutorial facts of the case, nor should he yet, having just been through a heart attack.

"I'm sorry," Hanson said.

"It's too hard to imagine Kyle—*my* Kyle; the one I have known for over twenty years. Best kid I ever knew. Grown to the best *man* I know. To imagine *this*?"

"It's only one option," said Hanson. "The insanity plea. It's early. We still have some time."

"But could you *win*? With an insanity defense."

"I honestly don't know," Hanson said. "Every trial depends on elements that are unrelated to the facts or the defense. Who finally sits in the jury box. What judge is assigned the case. It's almost a given that Kyle's going to be diagnosed as textbook PTSD. But that will be what our experts will say. The State will call experts to refute such a possibility."

"So it comes down to the jury," Pruett said.

"It *always* comes down to the jury, James. Always."

Wendy arrived a few hours after the phone call with Hanson was complete. The attorney was already in Cheyenne, waking up judges, pulling in favors, and doing everything possible to get an extension of the Grand Jury convening.

"Oh, god, Dad," Wendy said as she charged into his room and threw her arms around him.

"Good Lord, girl, how fast did you drive?"

"I called Lieutenant Fields at the Highway Patrol office back in Laramie. He's in the waiting area with everyone else."

"That's my daughter."

"What is Doc Percy saying?"

"He just moved me into this room, which means he's taken me off the 'officially endangered' list."

"But it was a heart attack?"

"A mild, myocardial infarction," said Pruett. "Brought on by an arterial blockage that requires no surgery."

"Good Lord."

"He said I'll be outta here tomorrow or the next day, Wendy. Two CAT scans and an MRI. So far, he's seen no damage."

"Thank God."

"One or two days ain't going to be enough," said Pruett.

"What the hell are you thinking?"

"Jail break."

> "If you do not change direction,
> you may end up where you are heading."
>
> ~Lao Tzu

Chapter 7

LIEUTENANT MANDY Jones walked over to the desks of the two detectives, Burnstead and Wilkins. "Mr. Yoder's attorney is here."

"Yoder wasn't about to give us anything anyway," Wilkins said.

"Speak for yourself," said Burnstead. "I'd love a chance to get him to talk."

Jones laughed. "Guy's been trained—and survived—Delta Force, Burnsy. You're the toughest cop I know, but you couldn't get his high school girlfriend's phone number unless he wanted you to have it."

"Your confidence in me is refreshing," the detective replied.

"Gotta go with the LT on this one, Greg. Those guys are for real, gung ho, nothing phases them, *bad-asses*," said Wilkins.

Burnstead only shrugged.

The lieutenant left the detectives to ponder the matter and went into his office. He returned a minute later with a tall, narrow man who didn't look like *he* could break his way out of a Styrofoam coffee cup.

"Detectives, this is attorney J.W. Hanson. He is now the attorney of record for Mr. Yoder and you will afford him all the respect that comes with that relationship."

"Detectives," Hanson said, extending a hand to Burnstead first.

Burnstead stood from his chair, immovable as granite, and placed his hands in his pockets.

"Detective," said Jones.

The burly cop removed a hand and accepted the gesture, sullenly. "Burnstead."

Wilkins was more receptive, but still with a defiant look. "Detective Charles Wilkins."

"Glad to meet you both," said Hanson. "Gentlemen—Detectives—I am not here, though you will believe otherwise, to be your adversary. Mr. Yoder has rights, and the facts of this case have not fully come to light."

"The facts of this case, *counselor*, are that your client murdered four innocent civilians," Burnstead countered.

"The police have the luxury of assuming one stance or the other—specifically, guilty," Hanson said, politely, still maintaining a veneer of calm and civility. No reason to turn on the adversarial until he had weighed the personalities with which he was dealing. "I'm here, clearly, to assume innocence first. That doesn't mean I'm against finding the truth. However, my client deserves an ally in his corner."

"An 'ally'," said the gruff detective. "Get a load of this."

"Detective," said the lieutenant. "Enough. Mr. Hanson, our department is after the same—the facts and truth of what occurred."

Lieutenant Jones motioned toward the interview room door.

Hanson pointed to the next door down, the one to the observation room. "May I?"

The lieutenant nodded. Hanson opened up the room, which was dark, and closed the door. "I assume cameras are turned off currently."

"I'll make sure they are," said the lieutenant, his own veneer beginning to show signs of weakening.

Hanson nodded, knocked lightly on the interview room door, and entered, closing the door and leaving the detectives and lieutenant behind.

~

Yoder looked up, disheveled, his exhaustion plain to see.

"Who are you?" he said, surprising Hanson by speaking first.

"Your new attorney," Hanson said, purposefully neutral and direct.

"Hmm," said Yoder. "Didn't know I was getting one."

"James Pruett hired me," Hanson said. Yoder perked up.

"Sheriff Pruett?"

"I'm engaged to his daughter."

Yoder then looked up, with hints of passion behind the steely exterior. For the first time, he locked eyes with Hanson. "Wendy?"

"Yes."

"*You're* engaged to Wendy?"

"Miracles still never cease," said the attorney, his ego stung by the young man's clear incredulity. "May I sit?"

Yoder didn't answer, looked away again, this time a bit dazed.

Hanson sat across the table. He noticed for the first time the shackles, securing Yoder to the metal table. Before saying anything more, the attorney stood up again and rapped on the inside of the door. Lieutenant Jones opened it.

"Can I get these restraints removed," Hanson asked, quietly.

"They're procedure," said Jones. "With any violent suspect—"

Still keeping his voice low, Hanson said with determination: "Lieutenant, with all due respect; my client has shown no propensity for violence from arrest until now. I've read the report and the file. You can't treat him like this because of his history; only current facts."

The lieutenant weighed the words and entered the room. He produced a key and unlocked the cuffs, leaving the chains in place but freeing Yoder. The ex-Delta soldier said nothing, only rubbed his wrists.

"Thank you, Lieutenant," Hanson said, as Jones left the room.

"It will be on record this was your request."

"Understood," the attorney acknowledged.

Hanson reentered the room and sat again.

"You get extra kudos over the previous guy," said Yoder, still rubbing his reddened wrists.

"If that's a *thank you*, you're welcome," said Hanson. "You seem different than James has described you these past years."

"How long have you known the sheriff?"

"A while. Around six years."

"Since his wife died," said Yoder.

"Yes."

"How long have you known Wendy?"

"Son, they probably aren't going to give us a lot of time. I need to discuss the situation with you."

"We've got until oh-nine hundred hours," Yoder said. "Then they dress me in orange, transport me to the courthouse, and my arraignment begins."

"But you and I need to talk before that happens," said Hanson. "I need you to speak with me as your attorney; I need your trust. Everything we discuss is between the two of us."

"Is Sheriff Pruett coming," Yoder asked. "I should have gotten in touch with him right when I got back. Strangest thing, though, at the time, he was the *last* person I wanted to see. Looking back now—"

"He's on his way," said Hanson. "You know he's not—"

"Sheriff anymore? Yeah. I know. But he'll never be anything else to me. That election was ridiculous. There's only one sheriff for Wind River, and Pruett is it. Not some candy-striper pretender without the skills to police himself much less the county, or even Wind River."

"Can't say I don't agree with you, Kyle. But we've got more pressing matters."

"It's crazy. I dedicate my life—even before enlistment—to what I believe to be noble service to my country. And now, *because* of my training—and really nothing else—I am going to be tried not only as a murderer but facing the *death penalty*?"

"What happened in that alley, Kyle?"

"When is Sheriff Pruett supposed to get here?"

"Probably within a few hours. He'll be here before your arraignment."

"I want to talk with him first."

"Kyle, I'm always going to be upfront with you. It's not going to be easy to get him in here. As your attorney, I have access. They don't have to allow James any access to the facility outside visitation, and currently you don't have visitation privileges."

"Then there's your first challenge, Mr. Hanson. I want to talk to Sheriff Pruett."

Pruett and Wendy arrived at the CPD main station, Division One, at six in the morning, deciding to wait until they went to their "hotel." When he'd first got to town, Hanson called in a favor with a friend whose house had for several years been used by the man and his wife as a Bed and Breakfast, called "The Paisley House" in reference to its original owner and once Cheyenne socialite Alberta Paisley. They would rent out rooms upstairs during the high tourist season. It got to be too much work as the two got older, cooking and cleaning for guests who treated the place like a Motel 8, so the couple got out of the B & B business and never used the second floor for much anymore.

Hanson's friend and his wife lived in a sectioned-off part of the downstairs and the upstairs had three bedrooms with two baths. Two of the bedrooms shared a bathroom, so Hanson talked his friend into letting Pruett stay in the room that used the lone bathroom and he and Wendy in one each of the bedrooms.

The feeling was that the house would be the "war room" for them for however long they needed. This way it gave them the entire upstairs.

~

Pruett approached the front desk and asked to speak with Chief Ewan Wallace.

"Do you have an appointment, sir?"

"No. I realize it's early, and the time crunch he's under, but this is regarding last night's events, and he's expecting my arrival. If you could tell him that James Pruett is here, I'd greatly appreciate it, ma'am."

"Please give me a few moments, Mr. Pruett. You can have a seat over there," the desk sergeant said, motioning to a row of empty chairs.

Pruett and Wendy sat down.

"I should call Jay and let him know we're here," Wendy said.

Pruett nodded, his thoughts elsewhere.

Wendy dialed Hanson's cell but it went to voicemail.

"No answer," she said.

"He could be interviewing him," said Pruett. "I want to talk to Wallace first, but we need to get over to county holding as soon as we can."

The desk sergeant caught Pruett's attention and waved him over.

"Chief Wallace instructed me to have you and your companion escorted to his office. Here are two visitor badges. Please keep them on at all times, above the waist."

"Wendy," Pruett said.

She walked over and clipped on her own yellow badge with a large "V."

"Please step over to the door and I'll buzz you in."

The two of them followed another officer who introduced herself as "Fredericks," to the elevator. They rode in silence to the top, 3rd floor, and got out. Fredericks escorted them down the hallway to the end, through a set of large glass doors, and into the reception area of the chief.

The chief's assistant looked up and smiled politely as they walked through. Officer Fredericks stopped at the open oak door of the chief's. Pruett and Wendy walked in.

Chief Wallace was at the far end of a good-sized office and when he saw them enter, he stood and came from behind his desk in one grand motion and covered the distance between them in two long strides. He put his arms around Pruett in a mighty hug, patting him on the back ferociously.

"James Pruett," he said. "Damn, how long has it been?"

Pruett returned the hug and said, "A long while, Chief. Too long."

"Dammit, James, you call me Ewan." He turned to Wendy. "Good Lord, this can't be Wendy."

"Pleasure to meet you, Chief Wallace," Wendy said nervously.

Wallace ignored her extended hand and gave her a polite hug. "Little lady, we've met before. I knew you when you wouldn't have reached your father's gun belt—which I'm betting this occasion to be one of the first he's without it."

"Well it's nice to put a face with the name, then," Wendy said.

"Same for you, too. It's Ewan or nothing at all," the chief said, smiling broadly.

"Ewan."

"Please come over and sit down, the both of you."

Pruett and Wendy sat in two low-back chairs and the chief across the desk in his own. Wallace looked over to where Officer Fredericks had closed the door, giving them necessary privacy.

"I wish this visit were otherwise in nature," Wallace said.

"No more than we do, Ewan," said Pruett. "But you and I both know we can't change the situation, or what it is."

"When we *know* exactly what it is," Wallace said.

"This has all happened very fast," agreed Pruett.

"Where y'all staying," asked Wallace, giving them his best Wyoming drawl. It was more than a little unimpressive.

"We're over at the old Paisley place," Wendy said. "Or will be, after our stop here."

"That's the B & B downtown?"

"Used to be," said Pruett. "People who own it are friends of a friend."

"Good. Tough to get rooms these couple of weeks."

"Maybe not for much longer," growled Pruett. He hadn't come to talk about the history of The Paisley House or tourist numbers.

"We should get to it," Wallace said.

"Amen," said Pruett.

Wallace looked over to Wendy and back to Pruett. "No offense whatsoever to Wendy; should you and I have a private talk, James?"

"Ewan, I trust my daughter with my life. There are no secrets between us. But it's your call. You're the chief."

Wendy held up her hand, not unlike a child asking permission to speak in the classroom. She did not wait, however:

"Chief—Ewan? No offense taken. I need to speak to our attorney and I think it would serve both purposes better, given the shortness of time, if you and my father stayed here, pissing your lines in the snow, and I can go and do what I need to do."

She gave neither man time to answer, picked up her shoulder bag, and smiled that *Wendy Pruett* smile—the one her old man knew left a person in a quandary; not as to whether or not *she* liked them, but rather how *they* should feel about her.

"We'll speak again, I'm sure, Ewan," she added, kissed her father on the cheek, turned on a dime, and walked effortlessly and without a sound out of the office. She even closed the door behind her, politely and softly.

Wallace looked at Pruett; the chief's countenance all sagging jowls and eyes, reminiscent of the hound dog that's been punished. "I truly meant it when I said I didn't intend offense," he managed.

Pruett smiled warmly. "Ewan, you didn't offend anyone. And the day I figure out my daughter and her machinations, you'll be the first I call."

"I told you before—told your deputy. Uh, ex-deputy. Damn I can't get used to that situation in Wind River."

"Try it on from my side," said Pruett.

"Can't imagine it," the chief admitted. "But you know what I said, and it still stands."

"I appreciate it. I've learned that you deal with things as they come your way. Day by day."

"Well we need to talk about the day-to-day *here*. You know the deal, James. I can't be running two investigations. We're not even twelve hours into this and the D.A. is making like she's got this case in the bag."

"There's not a lot going in favor of Kyle right now," Pruett said.

"No. But there's a missing part to this machine. Unfortunately they still haven't allowed a cop's gut into evidence."

"Understood. That's like the old saying, though: *just because I'm paranoid doesn't mean they aren't after me.*"

"What the hell are you talking about, Pruett?"

"Just because you can't admit gut feelings or reactions, doesn't mean they're wrong. How long *have* you been slumbering behind that chief's desk?"

"Same amount of time you been lounging up there in the high country as County Sheriff."

"Fair enough."

"Well *that* was too damn easy. When did you become so sunny-side-up?"

Pruett smiled. "Shit, chief. There is no sunny-side."

Wendy finally got through to Hanson. "Jesus, Jay, I've been calling for two hours. I left you three messages while we were on the road."

"Hello to you, too," he said.

"Sorry. I'm not good like this. With things in the dark, no pun intended."

"It's all right. I'm just leaving the county jail."

"You talked to Kyle?"

"He's not saying much. He wants to talk to your dad."

"And how do you propose we accomplish that feat?"

"I'm not worried about that one. Or let's say it's not at the top of the *priorities* list. I need to meet with D.A. Forster. Our one shot at maybe plea bargaining these charges before the arraignment."

"You aren't considering a plea deal, are you?"

"It's really more of a fishing expedition to see where the D.A. stands, but even though it's not the number one option, it's way too early to not keep all possibilities on the table."

"What can I do?"

"You and Pruett meet me at the house in an hour."

"Dad is with Chief Wallace right now."

"No new earth-moving news there, I'll assume."

"Doubt it," Wendy said. "They were doing the usual marking of territory and I figured it was a waste of my time right now to be sitting around listening to them banter and set the boundaries of this off the books investigation."

"I'm heading to the new courthouse now. To the district attorney's office."

"I'll head over to The Paisley House. Should I knock or what?"

"Tom said they'd leave a key in a magnet container under the mailbox right of the front door. They have the garage in back and enter and leave at the rear of the house."

"Sounds fine. I'll see you over there."

"Love you—" Hanson said, but to dead air.

~

The new Laramie County Courthouse was a remarkable building, although its contemporary design—architecturally striking as it was—did look somewhat out of place with the older brick veneer of the town.

Hanson entered the lobby, open but with no one at the reception desk yet, so he went to the elevator bank and pressed the button for the ninth floor. The elevator started moving.

The lawyer had expected a locked building, security stopping him—all manner of closed doors in his face. It seemed the entire town was off kilter with the imbalance of such a storm having turned to put Cheyenne in its path.

He got off at the ninth floor and saw a large office area with a singular glow coming out into the rest of the dim nighttime lights that still lit the early morning office area. Hanson walked down and opened the tall glass doors. He proceeded to the office with the lights on.

"Maggie Forster," Hanson said, as lightly as he could so as not to startle her. She jumped anyway.

"Oh, damn," she cried, and put her slender hand over her chest. She looked up to see who was there. "Jay Hanson. Now why am I not surprised to see you here, despite the hour?"

"We need to talk," said Hanson.

"I'd say that's an understatement. How long has it been?"

"Don't pretend you haven't entertained the idea that I might come over the mountain to represent this young man. Particularly with the family affiliation."

"So you'll be filing a motion to replace the public defender?"

"Maggie."

"It *is* up to the discretion of both the district attorney and the presiding judge if a change in counsel is necessary."

"Seriously? This is how we're going to begin the dance? You know there's a timer on all this, just as I do. Don't let our past make you venomous."

"Any way you want to spin it, it's a damn poor excuse for sneaking in and scaring a person half to death."

"There wasn't any sneaking. But I *do* need to see you. I would think you'd want to see me right about now."

"There you go, dripping with that Hanson ego. Sit down"

Hanson sat in a comfortable chair facing the D.A. She was a beautiful woman; the kind of beauty that first comes off as plain because it requires no extra makeup or attention to catch your eye and is a sin to cover too much.

"I assume you're here to discuss a possible plea bargain?" said Forster.

"Among other things I hoped to discuss with you."

"Let me see how good I still am at the conjecture game," Forster said coolly.

Hanson and she had attended Fordham Law College together for the final two of his three years. He'd not mentioned the fact to Wendy, not because there was really anything to hide, but there had been a time when Hanson foolishly thought he cared for the shrewd, intelligent, lawyerly woman.

There was a weekly challenge in their class on criminal prosecution where students would be given a collection of facts surrounding a case on Monday and, on Friday, present an educated speculation on both the defense and prosecution's primary strategies.

The exercise had been called *methodical conjecture*. Most of the students called it *Fortune-Telling 101*, but never to their professor's face or in his ominous presence.

"You were always the best at that exercise," Hanson said. "Please."

"You are only hours into being the attorney for Mr. Yoder. You have no witnesses, no defense, and thus no bargaining power. So you came here to *charm* your client's way off the lethal injection table."

"As merciful as ever," said Hanson. "I have a decorated war hero—one handed his *Medal of Honor* by the President of the United States of America. I have a defendant with absolutely no criminal record and no witness to refute his having never laid a finger on anyone, his entire life, much less *harmed* anyone. You, Maggie, have no motive. None. Your case is the definition of circumstantial."

"So it comes down to the jury. Are they a panel of simpering patriots or a gang of radical liberals, ready to light the flag on fire and have a weenie roast?"

Hanson smiled, then laughed.

"Finally, the fun Jay that I knew back in law school."

"We never had that much fun," said Hanson.

"That's because you were too afraid of me—afraid of what my answer would be."

"Your answer to what question?"

"Are we really going to play twenty questions, Jay? Is it bigger than a breadbox? Is it an animal? Will she say 'yes' if I ask her on a date?"

"And the lady gets the prize in three questions."

"You can be flippant," she said, almost purring. "But I would have said yes."

"As I recall, your routine included intentionally ignoring me every other morning as we walked the same route to Economic Law, found the furthest seat from me, and then ignored me on the route back until we split for different classes."

"See, the way I remember it, I was playing hard-to-get and kept wishing you'd break through that introverted shell and talk to me."

"I guess things worked out the way they were supposed to," he said.

"Did they," Maggie Forster asked. "Are you married?"

"Divorced. A-and engaged. Which I assumed you knew."

"I never married," she said. "Well, I did, but the law was my groom. And I did hear about your engagement. What is she, a friend of a niece?"

"Nice pot shot. A bit too much like fish in a barrel for someone of your standing, though. My first marriage was over before it really got started," he said, feeling as if the heat had been turned up a dozen clicks. "I practiced law for—"

"Twenty-two years," said Forster. "I kept tabs on you. You had a nice run there for a while. New York defense attorney; the *big time*."

"People try to pin that personality on me. I was simply a hardworking lawyer and did well with a lot of cases."

"You did better than well."

"As with everything, we are what the media makes us. In New York City, you can fall from grace quicker than overnight. But if you win, well, the stage is bigger and the spotlight finds you."

"I'm feeling like I should be intimidated," said Forster.

"You should consider discussing a plea agreement."

"Is that your opinion as law professor or defense attorney?"

"Both."

"You want to know the only thing that ever intimidated me about you?"

"Okay," said Hanson.

"That you lived in Laramie—less than an hour away—for more than ten years, yet never once came across the mountain to check on me."

"There never is a good time
for tough decisions...
...You have to pick courage and do it.
Governance is about taking tough,
even unpopular, decisions."

~Jairam Ramesh

Chapter 8

PRUETT DIALED the number from his stored contact list. He didn't know if it was even a good number for Dillon "Grinder" Roberts anymore. After the war, Pruett tried to stay in touch with as many of his platoon that survived the war. Sadly, there wasn't a long list of names to begin with, and as people scattered their different directions and one year became ten, the list grew smaller.

Some men really didn't want to remember their time in Vietnam, and to talk to a person who reminded you of the most horrific time in your life—even when that person was a friend; a man into whose safeguarding you once handed your life, and into your hands, he entrusted his own—well, it was simply understood. If men wanted to stay connected, remain friends, then it would happen.

And if they didn't, then that didn't happen. Numbers changed, people moved, some died—it was a strange dichotomy, the feelings of wanting and never wanting to see men who had once been closer to you than any before or since.

"Grinder" and Pruett didn't exactly stay close, though they had been very tight during the war. Roberts was one of the men, like Whitefeather, who cleaved to the camaraderie. Pruett, Grinder, Jeff Yoder, Malcolm Whitefeather, Johnny "Sage" Williams—"Sage" because he believed he could predict which new guys were going to make it and which weren't.

And Billy "Copper" Ruffalo—"Copper" not because of his hair, which was black and shaved tight to his skull, but because he *hated* the snakes. All kinds, large and small, poisonous or not. He would call them all "Coppers", since back home—Alabama—was "chock full" of copperheads.

Yeah, it was a scary, scary time, but Jimmy Pruett had survived, and a big part of the reason he did—mentally, at least—was due to the bonds of war.

Pruett last knew that Grinder Roberts was living somewhere in southern Colorado, moving around a lot. He wouldn't have known even that much, nor would he have had a number for Roberts, but Pruett ran into his old Army pal years back, when he made regular trips to Denver for various law enforcement conventions and training events.

On one of those trips, Pruett ran into Dillon Roberts in southern Metro Denver, near Franktown, in a bar called The Windpiper. The timeframe was in the thick of the sheriff's drinking years, and while at most of the conventions, the attendees mostly picked hotels close to the venue—usually in the downtown area—Pruett would normally choose a hotel in a more outlying area.

Truth happened to be that Pruett wasn't capable of going out for drinks with the boys. He'd tried that once and it didn't go over well—the uncontrolled drunk and the roomful of law enforcement personnel: city, county, state, and federal.

Not exactly a *toss back the shots* crowd.

Yet even though Pruett couldn't go "out for a drink," neither was he capable of *not* going out for drinks. He thought about simply ordering a bottle of Jack Daniels or Jim Beam from room service; sit in front of the television and drain his poison, alone in the room, but too often other cops dropped by, and Pruett couldn't trust what he might do after polishing off a fifth of eighty-proof booze.

So when the solution came to him, it was an epiphany of simplicity. The second year of conference attending, he feigned an administrative screw-up that had him staying at a hotel north of Denver proper. Denver, he'd learned, was the kind of city where you could stay anywhere and be twenty minutes from everything, and Pruett was a master functioning alcoholic. The man could stay up all night, or snatch a few hours of sleep, drain a pot of dark coffee, and make it through multiple days of boring lectures on the latest widgets or procedures of his profession.

He'd then slip out a little before the end of the last presentation or class, and simply desert the pack after the day's events. At first, it caused a few raised brows, but after setting precedent, Pruett just hinted that there was a special "someone" and this was his time of year to "vacation from the nest."

And so began what Pruett thought of as his love affair with his out-of-town lady, the bottle. Honestly it had always perplexed and perturbed him that a group of men could be so goddamned judgmental about his drinking habits, or lack of control thereof, yet give him the winks and the nods when they thought he was off to cheat on the wife.

"Yeah," a voice answered on the other end of the cell call, snapping the bad memories.

"Uh, yeah, looking for, uh, Grinder," Pruett said. He didn't recognize the voice.

"Who's looking?"

"Uh, James—Jimmy—Pruett."

A short silence and then: "*Jimmy Pruett? What the fuck, amigo? Call me out of the blue, shit, what's it been? Ten years? More?*"

"Probably more," said Pruett.

"Damn," said Roberts. "I wasn't sure I'd ever hear from you again after we *tore it up* at The Windpiper."

"That was a good night," lied Pruett, although it was *always* good to see someone from the 'Nam. Something about getting back together—planned or not—and it was like you were back in the bush, doing whatever passed for happiness back in that hellhole.

"What gives? You still *Sheriff* Jimmy Pruett? You call to bring me in for my bounty?"

Pruett had discovered that Grinder, as everyone knew him during the war, had more than an interest in motorcycles, as he told them then. He was Vice President of the Colorado chapter of the Lords of Mayhem, a bona fide, hardcore, motorcycle club, and the bar Pruett had chosen at random was one of the notorious biker bars in the area.

"Still sheriff when I'm up in Wyoming, at work. Not on duty now."

"You down here in the 303?"

"Actually up in Cheyenne," Pruett said. "But I don't make it over this close to Denver as much. Figured I would give you a shout."

"Man, it's good to hear your voice, JP."

"You, too, Grinder. I've missed you. Miss all the guys. You know how it is."

"Yeah, man, I do. Hey, what say I make a ride up north and come see you? We can have a beer and shoot the shit about the old, rockin' and rollin' days of the 'Nam."

"I'd like that," Pruett said. "When can you come?"

"Daaaaamn," said Grinder. "You sure you aren't here to bring me in, Sheriff."

"No way. Your life is yours, amigo. That's the pact. You remember."

"Yeah, JP, I remember. Sage, Copper, Yode, Whitefeather—hey, you still see that crazy old injun?"

"Absolutely. He lives near me now, up in Wind River."

"Malcolm, man, he's good people."

"The best."

"Alright, it's—shit—seven in the morning. What? Aw, never mind, JP. I'd ride up any time to see you. I can be up there in a couple of hours. Where you want to meet?"

"You tell me," Pruett said. "I'm new around here."

"Out by the Interstates, where I-25 and I-80 come together. There's a truck stop called The Outlander or some such shit. You can't miss it. Big 76 sign. Anyway, if you go north on the city street, uh, Timber, I think. Go down about a quarter mile, couple a stop signs, there's a shady little place called the Ride and Grill. Opens at dawn; a lot of old drunks sit there all day and spend their social security. Late at night the bikers take over."

"I can find that."

"Goddamn. Jimmy Pruett. I'll see you there, JP."

~

Pruett immediately started to get nervous. He hadn't thought any of it through. What, he was going to hang out at a biker bar with the Vice President of one of the most feared outlaw MCs in the southwest and order a sweet tea with lemon? And that was just for starters. Was he crazy? Could he really be considering talking to Grinder Roberts about—?

His cell rang and he pressed the answer button. "Pruett."

"Boss."

It was Red Horse Baptiste. "Red Horse, where are you?"

"Me and, uh, well, we're following up on that lead. The missing girl, Allison Chapman."

"Who's with you?" In the background, Pruett heard a muffle *let me talk. I can make my own decisions where I go and what I choose to do.* "Red Horse, you didn't."

"Boss, you know he's smarter than the two of us put together."

"And four times as rascally," Pruett said. "Put him on."

"Don't be cussin' out one injun for what you ought to be saying to the other," said Malcolm Whitefeather. "Baptiste, he came by and asked me if I wanted to help out. He told me about Kyle. I love that boy, too, Pruett. Hurts *you* didn't ask for my help."

"Things went down kind of fast, Mal. I had a heart attack, you know."

"I was right there in the waiting area, with all your friends."

"I know you were. I'm just sayin' a lot of things happened at once. Too fast for an old poke like me."

"You're forgiven. Now you want an update or not?"

"Yes."

"Allison Chapman is not at her apartment."

"Top notch investigative work, Whitefeather. Remind me not to hire you for my agency."

"Ah, shit, you know I'm pulling your leg, Jimmy. So we talked to several neighbors. She hasn't been back at all, or at least no one has seen her—and apparently, when she's around, *someone* knows about it. Not the quiet type. Plus she drives an old beat-up rice-burner, makes a shit ton of noise with that."

"Any leads?" Pruett said, still worrying about his meeting with Grinder.

"The guy who lives below her—I think he has a thing for her. Anyway, he said there is a rough boyfriend who comes over. Sometimes he stays there; sometimes she stays over at his place. We got an address, so me 'n Baptiste, we're going over to see if she might be hanging out there."

"Just keep this on the low-down, okay, Mal?"

"Already got the lecture from Baptiste on the way over here from Wind River. Makes an old injun wonder what ever happened to respecting the elders and all that tradition."

"Unfortunately I don't think tradition plays well these days, my friend."

"You got that right. Stay safe, Jimmy," Whitefeather said, and disconnected.

Yeah, thought Pruett. *Stay safe.* He looked at his watch. He still had over an hour and a half until he was supposed to meet Roberts.

He dialed Wendy's cell, figuring Hanson might still be with the D.A.

"Sheriff?" Wendy answered.

"Damn, I love it when you call me that, darlin'."

"It's who you are, in case you needed any reminding."

"Where are you?"

"I talked to Jay a while ago. I'm driving to the house. He needs us to meet him there in about an hour."

"All right," Pruett said. "I'll be over there shortly."

~

At The Paisley House, neither Hanson nor her father seemed to have arrived, so Wendy parallel parked on the street, leaving room for the other two, and walked up to the front door. She fished around and beneath the mailbox and found a thin rectangle with a top that slid open. Inside were a house key and a note:

Please help yourself to the kitchen. We stocked the fridge and pantry.
Tom & Jolene

Wendy went back for her travel bag and came back up to the house. She unlocked the door and stepped into 1867. She was in the middle of a grand, rounded anterior room, with polished redwood floors and dark, maple planked walls, all trimmed in a spectacular white. The doors between rooms were large, with magnificent archways; they, too, were painted pristine white. And the front of the first floor was filled with antique furniture in unblemished condition.

Finally, the staircase wound up the right wall, following the curve of the room, with widely spaced round dowels topped by a lathed, white rail.

The house was the prettiest Wendy had ever seen. She walked through the archway on the left, into a main dining area with a long, wooden table with a thin, flower-patterned cloth and ten high back, matching chairs. There was a fireplace back in the center of the room with a tall, brick hearth and on the opposite wall a bookcase that ran from floor to ceiling, filled with hardback books.

Wendy heard a soft rap before the front door slowly opened. She walked back around to find her father.

"Wow," said Pruett, removing his hat. "Feel like I should take off my boots."

"It's amazing," Wendy said.

The two of them carried their luggage upstairs, where the ample floor space was just as impressive, no longer wooden walls but, rather, plaster, painted a neutral earth tone of off-white.

The beds were each high-framed, with four posts and thick, feathery comforters.

Downstairs the front door opened again and Jay Hanson came up the staircase two steps at a time.

"Did I say it was gorgeous?" he said when he found them in the back bedroom.

"You didn't lie," said Pruett. "I don't normally go for the frilly, but this place is one of a kind."

"Feels like we should be paying for the tour," said Wendy. "Like it'd be a sin to mess anything up."

"Ah, it's still just a house," said Hanson, sitting down on one of the beds. "Though they don't build them like this much anymore."

"Not to bust up the party," said Pruett. "But I'm meeting with an old friend that might help in the investigation. Want to fill us in, Professor?"

"Well, we're not going to get any deals from the prosecutor," Hanson said. "Not that we were really looking for one, but I can tell you she is confident in her position." He opened his briefcase and produced two single pieces of paper. He handed Pruett the first one. "Sign it."

Pruett looked at the legal paragraphs and saw "Business shall heretofore refer to *Pruett Investigations, LLC.* of Wind River, Wyoming."

"What is *this*?"

"It's an official hiring form from the law office of J.W. Hanson. You, sir, are my newly hired investigator."

"Oh, I am? I don't remember applying for the position," said Pruett. "What's the job pay?"

"Not much for now, I'm afraid," said Hanson. "But it allows your presence at all attorney-client interviews."

The light went off in Pruett's head. "You son of a—this gets me in to see Kyle."

"And, more importantly, gives me an expert set of eyes and ears for finding out what we need to prove the man innocent. I didn't hire you for your good looks. I need your expertise, James."

Pruett was clearly caught up in the idea of seeing Kyle again. Hanson took the other piece of paper and handed it to Wendy.

"My offer of an internship at one of the finest law practices in the state of Wyoming, Ms. Pruett. Doesn't pay a lot, but gives you the full access of an assistant paralegal. I plan to file both documents this morning. We should be able to get you both in to see Kyle before the arraignment."

"You carry this paperwork around with you at all times?" Wendy said. "You *are* impressive."

"Printed last night at an Internet café from a site called 'PersonalLegal.com'. It's one of those places where every individual citizen can be their own lawyer and download forms from last will and testaments to divorce papers. Fortunately, they also have a decent collection of employment forms."

"Brilliant," said Wendy, and kissed Hanson deeply. "I knew I loved you for a reason."

Pruett handed the attorney his signed document. "Boss," he said, put on his hat, and tipped it to Hanson as he headed down the hallway.

"Where are you going?" said Wendy.

"Like I said, meeting an old friend. With my employer's permission, that is."

Of course, Pruett didn't wait for any as he loped down the stairs and out into the brightening morning.

Baptiste and Whitefeather slowed down the car and rechecked the address the neighbor from Allison Chapman's complex had given them.

"This is the place," said Red Horse.

"Not the best part of the town," Whitefeather observed.

Baptiste got out of the car. "You stay here. Keep an eye out for the girl. Let me see if I can find the boyfriend."

"Bullshit, Baptiste," said Whitefeather, getting out of the car. "I told you if I was comin', I was going to be part of the team, not just a third wheel."

Baptiste did not smile. "If things go bad, you stay out of it," the big man told him.

"I can handle myself."

The pair walked up to the duplex and climbed the dilapidated stairs.

"2507," said Whitefeather.

Baptiste ignored him and rapped on the door. There was a faint sound of movement from inside, but no one answered. The deputy knocked again, this time a bit louder. "Frank Hawkins," Baptiste said.

"Who is it?" responded a voice from the other side of the door.

"Wind River police," Baptiste said, improvising. "We need to ask you some questions."

The door opened and an unkempt man with tousled black hair, a white, sleeveless tank top exposing tattoos up and down his average arms, stood there, cigarette dangling from dry, cracked lips. He looked from one of the two back to the other.

"Wind River? What's this you say about *police*? This is Cheyenne, Tonto. You and your injun friend are on the wrong rez."

"Is that right?" Baptiste said, trying to remain professional, remembering Chief Wallace's admonition of *off the books*. "We're right where we want to be, Mr. Hawkins. We're looking for Allison Chapman."

"Now it's *Mr.* Hawkins. Look, Tonto. No comprende, okay? I have no idea who you're talking about anyway."

Baptiste had taken about all he was going to take. Whitefeather could see the patience draining in his friend and he stepped up, putting himself partially between the two of them.

"My name is Malcolm," he told Hawkins, and extended a hand that the scruffy man ignored. "We're not here for trouble. This is part of an investigation. Can you help us find Ms. Chapman? It's very important."

Frank Hawkins leaned forward and spoke right into Whitefeather's face, his breath a mixture of yesterday's booze and morning cigarettes. "No. Comprende."

Baptiste moved so quick Whitefeather didn't even have time to react. He lifted Hawkins well off the ground and carried him into the front room of the tiny living space. "Close the door," he said to Whitefeather, who did.

The big Nez Perce in the Stetson hat and blue jeans put the flailing man hard against the wall, keeping him off the floor with a forearm across Hawkins' neck and windpipe.

"My name isn't *Tonto* and my friend back there was a state agent of the Colorado Bureau of Investigations for twenty years, Hawkins. We don't speak Spanish. I'm Nez Perce and Mr. Whitefeather back there, he's Blackfoot. We don't *comprende* either."

"Lay off, man," Hawkins managed, half-choking to death. "Put me down."

"No, not a chance." Baptiste said, and leaned in real close, nose-to-nose. He spoke quietly, so Whitefeather wouldn't hear. "I know a dozen ways to kill you that don't require me to move more than a few inches. We came here, polite, and asked you a simple question. My suggestion would be that you *answer* it before I choose one of the twelve."

Hawkins struggled again, still with no success. Red Horse Baptiste was a strong man, and he knew how to control a prisoner. He pressed in on his captive's windpipe, just enough to steal a little more of that precious oxygen.

"She came by last night," the man squeaked. "Nervous. All wigged out."

Baptiste released some of the pressure to allow the man to speak. Hawkins sucked in air in big gulps.

"Jesus, man, don't kill me."

"Didn't come here to kill you," said Baptiste. "Finish your answer."

"I figured she was high on somethin'. She wasn't making sense. Kept saying 'the Army man, the Army man—killed those guys.' I told her Army dudes kill guys all the time. She said she had to take off, stay safe."

"So where did she go?"

"I don't *know*."

Baptiste pressed in harder. "I said we didn't come here to kill you. Doesn't mean we can't make a change of plans."

"Her parent's place," Hawkins managed. "I think she was going to go and crash in their basement."

The big deputy released Hawkins and he crumpled to the littered floor, rubbing his neck.

"Give us the address," was all Baptiste said.

~

Once they were back in the car, Baptiste removed his cell and dialed the number Chief Wallace had given him.

"Hello?"

"Chief, it's Deputy Baptiste."

"Call me back in five minutes."

The deputy waited and then called again.

"Sorry," the chief said when he answered. "I wanted to step out of the office. How are things going with the search for the girl?"

"We've got a lead that she may have gone to her parent's house," Baptiste said.

"Anything else?"

"Her boyfriend said she came in last night crazy afraid of 'the Army man'. Said he killed the victims."

"She's talking about Yoder. He was wearing a Ranger's jacket when he was found."

"Maybe," said the deputy. "We're going over to the address now."

"Yoder's not talking. He's already met with Hanson. I didn't get the impression the attorney got much out of him either."

"What are your detectives going to do?"

"The uniforms last night must not have come back with any information. Burnstead and Wilkins didn't say anything to me about a boyfriend."

"You want us to keep going?" It wasn't like Baptiste was going to stop either way, but it seemed like the right question to ask.

"Yeah. The detectives are due to call in with a status report in a few minutes. I'm not saying anything to them about the boyfriend or parents. I'll call you back on this number after the briefing."

"Roger that," said Baptiste, and disconnected.

"What did the chief say?" said Whitefeather.

"Nothing. The detectives didn't get anything on the girl last night."

"So we still heading to the parent's place?"

"Yep."

"That's it? *Yep?*"

Baptiste looked over at Whitefeather, whose eyes were on the road. "You want me to do a rain dance?"

Whitefeather shook his head. "Now that's just *wrong*, deputy."

Pruett found the *Ride and Grill*, right where Roberts told him it would be. He didn't see any bikes in the gravel parking lot, just one beat-up truck and a rundown Pontiac that looked like one of Pruett's first cars as a teenager.

He showed up early intentionally. Pruett wanted to think. He felt as if the torrent of events had swept him into the storm so quickly—the information about Kyle, the heart attack, horrific images of his godson facing insurmountable legal odds—Pruett just needed a minute or two alone to decompress, gather his senses, and consider the road down which he—a lawman, or at least one for most of his adult life—was about to travel.

There *were* things more important in life than the law. It wasn't as if Pruett was naïve enough to believe in absolutes. Laws, just as everything else put on paper to construct a manageable society, were important, applicable, and unbreakable for the majority of cases.

That didn't mean that the life of a family or friend—*an innocent one*—couldn't trump the almighty supremacy of law. But even such a stance, principled and tenable as it might be, applied only in the case of a person's *known* innocence.

Didn't it?

Was supposition good enough?

Was a policeman and godfather's *gut?*

This plan Pruett was concocting—this *BACKUP* plan—was way off any map known to Pruett. Every man or woman had bent their ethics, ignored an occasional moral or rule, when it came to protecting someone or something more important than said ethic, rule, or moral.

This wasn't rounding down on one's income tax.

This was as illegal and improper and *feloniously criminal* as it got. Pruett couldn't afford to go into this rationalizing or justifying *anything*. This was, plain and simple, breaking the law to save a young man's future—a young man Pruett believed with every fiber of his being could not be guilty of the crimes of which he was accused.

If Pruett stayed on this path—even *conspiring* such machinations—he felt as if he was putting a torch to ideals that he'd sworn to uphold.

Fuck it, Pruett thought. *Life just ain't that simple. There's no black and white. There's 'usually', and 'do the very best you possibly can', but there isn't ONE ANSWER to every conundrum we face. Lighten up.*

A man can tell a woman she ain't fat in jeans bursting along the seams but that does *not* make him a pathological liar. A poor example, maybe, but it still made the point: flexibility and compromise—even at the highest levels of morality and under the direst of circumstance—were as necessary to a fair civilization as were law, judgment, and punishment.

Pruett would be damned ten times over before he would leave the decision to pump poison into the veins of Kyle Yoder—godson, patriot, hero, and one of the *good guys*—up to twelve yokels from bum-fuck, Dustville, Wyoming.

He would stay, meet with his friend. He would lay out his fallback plan. And the chips, well, the fucking chips would fall where they needed to, but no innocent war hero was going to be put to death on James Pruett's watch, sheriff or not.

About ten minutes later he *heard* Roberts approach: from how many blocks away he didn't know, but it could have been miles. The coarse, feral growl of the Harley was unmistakable. As it approached, the mean purr of the bike made Pruett wish he'd never gotten rid of his. He was never a serious rider, but for a few years, he'd ridden the switchbacks above Wind River, cool wind in his hair, and had really enjoyed the bike.

Bethy had finally put the kibosh on that adventure. She worried about him too much, back then. Funny, but things such as the worry of a wife and her making him sell his prized motorbike; he'd take back in a moment if it meant he could have her back, too.

The Harley and its rider pulled up next to Pruett's rental car.

It was Grinder Roberts for sure, though—like Pruett, and all men—he'd aged. More pounds, grayer hair emergent from under his blue bandana, and more wrinkles. But it was clearly his old friend, albeit a brother from another lifetime; a ghost from the distant past.

Pruett opened the window of the car.

"Nice ride," said Roberts, his smile gleaming and genuine. Pruett figured there was at least a hundred grand of dental work inside his buddy's mouth. Whoever said crime didn't pay was simply a criminal who got *caught*.

"Yours, yeah," Pruett said. He got out of the car, his considerable frame difficult to maneuver out of the foreign model he'd gotten when they arrived in Cheyenne. "A softail, no?"

"Yep. Fat boy. I'll never ride anything else." Roberts climbed off his bike, jeans, boots, and a long sleeve hoodie beneath his leather, sleeveless MC jacket. He opened his arms wide and embraced Pruett. "Jimmy Pruett, all grown up."

"It's damn good to see you, Dillon."

Roberts patted him hard on the back. "You, too, amigo. You, too."

~

Inside the bar, the two grabbed a table. Pruett ignored his usual rule, but wound up facing the room by chance.

"Friendly place," said Pruett.

"You don't have to shit me, Jimmy. I am who I am, just like you."

"I didn't mean it that way—"

"I know you didn't. I just wanted to say it up front. Don't matter where or when I see you—or how old we get," he laughed. "It'll always be good. *Always.*"

"I feel the same."

"You seen any of the others," asked Roberts. "I mean besides Mal Whitefeather."

"Not really. You know how it is. People drop outta touch."

Roberts nodded, just as a rough-looking waitress sidled over.

"What'll you boys have? Kitchen ain't open. The usual for you, Grinder?"

"Yeah," he said. "Just soda water, Jill. Throw a lime in it for good luck."

"What about you, hon?"

"I'll have an iced tea, ma'am."

"Jilly, this is Sheriff James Pruett. We go way back."

"Nice to meet you, Sheriff. You want sweetener in that tea?"

"Sugar please. Nice to meet you, too, Jill."

The waitress walked away.

"She's good people," said Roberts. "I don't get up this way as much as I used to."

"I wanted to talk to you about something, uh, well, a delicate situation."

"Ha. What the hell is that supposed to mean?"

"Sorry, Dillon, it's not something I come to lightly or want to involve you in."

Roberts leaned closer. "Anyone else called me 'Dillon', Jimmy, and I'd probably cut out their tongue. You're family, brother, but call me Grinder."

"Sorry, Grinder."

"It may not roll off the palate like the old days, but that's all you used to call me."

"It'll work, long as you don't call me 'Sheriff'."

"Fair enough. But you are, ain't you?"

"Long story. Let's say I was forced into retirement."

"Damn. I know the feeling. I think my days as Prez of *The Lords* is probably coming to an end. Too old for the shit, Jimmy. Back in the day— in the bush—I thought we'd live *forever*."

"What do you do then, though? When you're not the man you've always been?"

"Shit, JP, I'll *always* be me. Grinder Roberts. No one will ever take that away."

"Over the years, after the war, I made the mistake of letting my job define me."

"We all get defined by our jobs," said Grinder. "Ain't no 'let' about it. That's life, JP."

"Yeah, but how do you get by when the job's done?"

"Then get your job back, bro. Or find another one."

"Maybe," said Pruett.

Jill the waitress brought them their drinks and walked away before Pruett could thank her. He figured it probably wasn't the kind of place where the help expected a lot of gratuity.

"Look at the two of us," said Grinder. "Iced tea and soda water."

"I had to give it up," Pruett said, more than a little embarrassed. "Fuckin' shit had me by the cajones, Grinder. It was kill or be killed."

"Me, too. My liver gave out," the biker said. "Sister gave me a piece a hers. I owe her now. Besides, takes a helluva lot tougher man to *not* drink."

"Amen to that," said Pruett, and the two clinked glasses.

There was a bit of a silence while the two cooled off with their drinks, then Grinder broke the tenuous still:

"Coulda knocked me over with a condom, gettin' a call straight outta the history books from Jimmy 'JP' Pruett."

"Yeah," said Pruett. "Wish I'd a reached out sooner, under better circumstances."

"Fuck that noise," said Grinder. "Hearin' your voice; might as well have been *yesterday*."

"Time flies, that's for goddamned sure," growled Pruett.

Grinder dropped his voice an octave. "Now what is this thing you have rolling around in your mind, filling that mouth of yours with marbles? Some plan has you remindin' me over the phone about our pact—our *blood oath*."

Before they all left 'Nam, the group of them—the survivors—swore to each other that, wherever, whenever, however they landed in life back in the States, and no matter how many years passed, if any one of them ever needed another—*EVER*—it would be a no questions asked, do whatever you can for your brother, kind of deal.

War bound people in strange ways, and it made brothers out of men who might not ever so much as share a table or a drink in civilian life. But the camaraderie of that group had been—was—as real as any friendship Pruett had known in his lifetime.

"There's a storm coming down on this town," Pruett said. "And my godson—Yode's boy; you remember when Yode died with his wife all those years ago—well Yode's kid, a man like a *son* to me, is about to be consumed by it. I've thought of every *legal* play I can make—every legal angle to get this poor kid out of gettin' a needle in his arm—and goddammit, Grinder, but I am *running out of options*."

"So you called me."

"Oh, man. Don't say it like that."

"Didn't mean it like that. Man needs a refrigerator fixed, he calls a refrigerator repairman. He needs a new liver, he calls the doctor. That's all I meant."

"So I called you. It's not right; not fair to put you and your MC in the middle of something—"

Roberts waved him off. "Don't. Don't do that. I don't take offense, nor do I hold anything against a man who is out to protect his family. In the end, it's all most men will ever have. I need to know what you want, Jimmy. What do you need me to do?"

"There's going to be a trial. And the investigation and evidence is not in our favor. Not by a long shot."

"When does this trial begin?"

"Grand Jury convenes at nine this morning. They'll indict, Grinder, sure as Charlie was in the shit, they'll indict."

"Then the kid gets arraigned, probably held without bail, and the trial gets rollin' in another week or two."

"You know the process better'n I do," said Pruett.

"I've been down that road," Grinder said. "More times than I wish."

"I was talking to Kyle's—that's Yode's boy—his attorney. First thing they'll do is pick a jury. I love Wyoming, Grinder. Only girl I ever loved more was my wife. But with the evidence against Kyle, I'll be damned straight to Hell if I'm going to leave his life in the hands of twelve idiots from God knows where."

"You know what they say," Grinder said, sipping at his soda water. "It only takes one."

"I've been over it a hundred times in my head," Pruett told his friend. "I just can't think of any other way—other'n *proving him innocent*, I mean."

"Can I ask you something?"

"Of course," said Pruett. "Anything."

"Are you sure he didn't do it?"

Pruett could not answer immediately, and it bothered him. "Sometimes you have to believe. The kid I knew—the one I half-raised? Not a chance in a million years."

"But the man?" said Grinder. "How many tours?"

"Four," said Pruett.

"Dammit."

"Did I mention he's Delta?"

"No," said the MC President. "I'd say that works in his favor. Not in a court of law, 'course, but in the mind of men who've been in the shit. You make it to Delta, you have a control of personal action few other men do."

"I tell you, Grinder. You get to know someone at his core, like I know Kyle Yoder, you know what he's capable of. I'm convinced he couldn't have done these senseless things. But I'm not sure my opinion changes of what *I* must be capable."

"Promises to a dead father," said Grinder.

"And the unconditional loyalty of a living one."

"Here's a number," Roberts said, writing it on a napkin and sliding it across the table. "When the jury's picked, you dial it. Ask for me."

"But—"

"Shit, JP, just call. Don't say anything else. I love you, man."

And the brother named Grinder got up, put on his sunglasses, and left the bar.

As Pruett listened to the loud snarl of the Harley pull away, he felt sick to his stomach. But he folded up the napkin and put it in his wallet anyway.

~

Outside in the parking lot, Pruett's cell rang.

"Yeah," he answered.

"It's Baptiste."

"What'd ya get, Red Horse?"

"Guy in the apartment underneath Rachel Chapman said she might be hidin' out with her parents on the other side of town."

"Give me the address. I'll meet you there."

"The healthy man does not
torture others - generally
it is the tortured that turn
into torturers."

~Carl Jung

Chapter 9

AS PRUETT pulled up in front of the suburban residence of Allison Chapman's parents, the car with his best friend and his ex-deputy was already waiting.

"Let's pull down over there, in front of the greenbelt. Since we're off the books on this investigation, I don't want any voyeurs placing us or our vehicles in front of the Chapman house."

Pruett and Baptiste pulled the cars down half a block and the three men exited the vehicles and walked back up to the target household.

What they found was a pair of cars parked in the driveway and the front door ajar—clearly forcibly opened. The deputy rang the doorbell anyway. There was no answer. He rang it again.

"This isn't right," said Whitefeather.

"No, it's not," agreed Pruett.

"Do we go in?"

The trio listened for any sounds from within the house. Baptiste rang the bell a third and last time. Nothing. No sounds at all. "They could be out."

"With both cars in the driveway and the front door busted open?" said Pruett.

"Have you considered what we might find in there?" Baptiste said. "This investigation is *off the books*, remember? How are we supposed to explain our presence here if we find something reportable?"

"What if someone inside needs help? We can't just walk away," Pruett said.

"No, we can't," said Baptiste. "Shit."

Pruett removed a small thirty-eight-caliber revolver from behind his back, where it had been slid into his belt. He moved past Baptiste and slowly opened the front door of the Chapman house. The tiled entryway opened into a large living area, with three carpeted steps up into the house.

"Hello? Police—call out if anyone can hear me," Pruett said, loudly. "Anyone."

No response.

The three men walked into the living room and moved toward the kitchen area. There were no signs of a struggle. Pruett and Baptiste cleared each of the rooms, first floor and second, while Whitefeather watched their backs.

"The boyfriend said something about her staying in the basement," Whitefeather said.

"Yes, we'll get there, Mal," said Pruett. He wasn't feeling good about what might be found on the lowest level.

They walked through the kitchen to a door that seemed likely to lead down to the basement. Pruett turned to Baptiste. "Stay behind me. If we find anything, you still stay put. I'm just a civilian, with nothing to risk, technically speaking. You're an officer of the law and can't afford to be identified as having been here. Agreed?"

Baptiste nodded.

Pruett started down the stairs. It was when he reached the second-to-last step that he saw the first of the blood trail in the carpet of the finished basement. He held his weapon steady, slowly turning the corner.

The husband and wife were in the middle of the room, duct-taped to a pair of chairs. They were not moving, not even their chests. From their discoloration, much of the blood having already begun to settle in their lower extremities, Pruett guessed they hadn't moved in quite a while.

"Stay on the stairs," he told Baptiste and Whitefeather. Pruett then slowly crossed the room on the balls of his feet, gun still ready, careful not to disturb the crime scene. When he reached the Chapmans—or who could only assume was the Chapmans—he tried to remain calm, but the beatings the two had suffered were profound.

Pruett reflexively reached out and checked each for a pulse. He didn't expect to find any, and he didn't. He noticed that Mr. Chapman had been burned at least a dozen times with some type of incendiary device.

As if the beatings hadn't been enough.

Pruett checked the small bathroom and downstairs bedroom, still being certain he did not tarnish the crime scene or leave any trace of their having been there. When he returned to the staircase, Malcolm Whitefeather looked whiter than a sheet of paper.

"We have to go," he told his friends.

All Whitefeather could manage was a nod. Baptiste said nothing and the three men retreated back the way they had come. They left the front door in the same position as they found it and walked down to their cars.

Pruett looked up and down the quiet neighborhood. There was no one outside; no cars driving on the street.

"Hurry up," he said to Baptiste and Whitefeather. "Get in the car."

"Those people—" Whitefeather said.

"Nothing we can do for those poor people in there," said Pruett. "But we need to leave before anyone sees us here. Wallace will be calling. We can report this crime anonymously."

The men got in their cars and sped away.

Pruett decided he wanted to give the information directly to Wallace. An anonymous tipster could trigger a whole other sub-investigation, and Pruett both wanted all the cards on the table and, most importantly, all the resource focused on who really killed the four men.

It wasn't like he had a lot of confidence in Wallace to do the job, but he didn't have a lot of choices. In fact, he didn't have *any*. Regardless of how the scene at the Chapman residence was reported, it was still going to end up rolled into the overall ongoing murder investigation.

And it wasn't as if there were twenty different crime labs or a dozen different medical examiners. Cheyenne was big by comparison but it was still a tiny town. They had different districts and jurisdictions for investigations, but all the work funneled back into a system with myriad bottlenecks. The process wasn't unlike that in most cities, but Cheyenne had only one of *everything*: Medical Examiner, toxicologist, ballistics expert, etc.

"What in Sam Hill do you mean *they're DEAD*?"

"We got to their house and the cars were in the driveway and the front door had been forced open."

"Do not say you went into the house."

"And what else would you have wanted me to do?" said Pruett, the anger starting to build. "You called us. If you don't want the truth, I don't know what to tell you."

"The Chapman's are *dead*," the chief said, as if repeating the words would change the fact. "Dead how?"

"The bodies are in the basement, taped to chairs. They were beaten badly and the man was tortured—burned with something. Someone was looking for information. Short leap as to what—or who—the killer was looking for."

"Did anyone see you?"

"I don't think so."

"You left things undisturbed?"

"No," said Pruett. "We dragged the bodies out to the front lawn and posed for photographs after the tabloids got there. We called them, of course."

"No cause for the attitude, James."

"You realize what this means, Ewan?"

"I've got six bodies and counting," Wallace said.

"Kyle couldn't have done this. He's in lockdown."

"Could be an accomplice."

"To a *homeless* guy? Who's never made contact with another person practically since he got home from Afghanistan?"

"It does help the defense, I'll give you that."

"Listen, you're not *officially* my boss, Chief. But we're in this together. I'm here to help, but not to take heat from you for doing my job, and doin' it as you asked."

"All right. What do you want to do? You've had more time to process this, this, *complete* insanity."

The chief sounded about ready to lose control. Pruett wanted to tell him to call off the farce and put the ex-sheriff in charge of the investigation. It wasn't like that was going to give him the right to start kicking down doors, but at the moment he felt like he was in a boxing match with one arm secured behind his back and rocks in his shoes.

"If you really want me to get out in front of this, why don't you deputize me or swear me in as some kind of a special task force investigator, give me some goddamned *authority*, and let's get some momentum behind this investigation."

He knew the impotency of the words before they were finished coming out of his mouth.

"Next year's an election year," Wallace said. "There's a head of steam building for me as a contender of Commissioner. I can't have it looking like I called in Yosemite Sam and Elmer Fudd from the smallest town in the country to solve the largest murder case in Cheyenne's history, *under my jurisdiction.* Uh, no offense—I was just trying to lighten the mood."

"Nah, I get it," Pruett growled. "But I'm done pussyfootin' around. There'll be no official announcements, and I'll keep it as quiet as I can, but you can at least come up with a story about needing reinforcements to do some of the lesser legwork of the investigation."

"Agreed," said Wallace. "But you gotta swear to me you'll keep this thing as tight as a duck's pucker."

"Watertight," said Pruett.

"What'd the big man have to say?" Whitefeather wanted to know.

"He doesn't know whether to shit or go blind," Pruett said. "But I made it clear that we were done tiptoeing around like church mice."

"GOOD," said Baptiste. "What's next?"

"You two go and report the Chapman house to Detectives Wilkins and Burnstead. Chief Wallace said he was calling ahead as I left to inform them that we'd been called in to assist in some of the less glamorous investigative details. We'll be answering to them, but they're up to their eyeballs in it, so as far as I'm concerned, this gives a *whole* lot bigger leash to work with."

Thursday, July 23rd 10:00 A.M.

J.W. Hanson walked Pruett up the stairs into the county jail facility as he'd been there twice before, both times escorting students from his law courses at the University of Wyoming, bringing them for a viewing of the criminal judicial process. The two men waited at the desk, where they signed in, and after being checked as approved-access in the computer system, eventually given large "V" badges that were green in color. A Laramie County Sheriff deputy then showed them where to wait to be escorted to the interview room.

Earlier Hanson had been informed that Kyle was being moved to county holding for the preliminary arraignment that followed the Grand Jury's indictment, as expected. County holding was simply a separate section of the county jail where inmates were held prior to appearance in court; the row of cells had access, through two sets of steel lockdown doors, to a hallway that led to a door in the back corners of several district courtrooms for defendants to be given access to the trial proceedings.

Another deputy eventually came in and escorted Pruett and Hanson through a door, and then down by the two lockdown slide doors, where they took a left down a long corridor with closed doors.

They were stopped in front of room B15.

"I'll be right out here," the deputy told them. "Just knock if you need out. We'll need to take the prisoner fifteen minutes before eleven. You can then go to the arraignment courtroom 'B' to see your client at the scheduled time."

"Is the docket running on schedule this morning," Hanson asked.

The deputy nodded. "So far." He then stepped in front of them and let them into the holding/interview room.

Kyle was seated at a table in the middle of the room, handcuffed to the table in an orange county jumpsuit with "LDOC" stamped on the left chest where a pocket might be on a normal shirt.

He'd been allowed to clean up, and had at least trimmed back his beard, but to Pruett he was still near unrecognizable.

"Sheriff," Kyle said, his voice most even, with a slight tremolo as he held back his emotions.

Pruett went across the room and leaned over to embrace his boy. "You look terrible," he said to Yoder. "But damn I've missed you, son."

They held the embrace, neither it seemed, wanting to release first.

"I should've called you when I got back," Kyle said.

Pruett stood up, his eyes wet, shaking his head. "You went where you needed to go. I knew you'd reach out when you were ready."

Kyle's eyes looked pleading. "I can't have done this, Sheriff. I just can't."

"We're gonna get it all straightened out," said Pruett. He and Hanson sat down across the table from Yoder. "This man here—Jay Hanson—he's my friend, Kyle. I've trusted the man with my family. You know how important that is to me. You *need* to put your trust in him."

Kyle nodded.

"Promise me, son."

"I promise."

Pruett turned to Hanson. "All right. Explain the arraignment again. You know this prosecutor. What should we expect?"

"Honestly, this is pretty short and standard," Hanson said. "The law requires that the State—the Laramie County District Attorney, in this case—read the charges against you in open court. Kyle, you'll simply be asked to acknowledge that you understand the charges as described to you."

"When do I get to speak?"

"You don't. What I mean is, you're not agreeing to anything. It's like the reading of your Miranda rights. Just acknowledge that you understand the charges as read to you. Then the judge will ask how you plead. You reply 'not guilty'."

"That's it?"

"Pretty much," said Hanson. "I'll make a request for bail exception but it will be denied and you'll be remanded—taken back—to the county jail."

"I can't get bail?"

"He's a *war hero*," Pruett said.

"Unfortunately in capital murder cases, bail is automatically denied."

"I thought you said the judge had the power to make an exception," Pruett said.

"Under extraordinary circumstances. And I told you I've never seen it happen. I wish it wasn't true, but I'm trying not to sugarcoat this. You're going to be held in jail until this trial is over, Kyle. I'm sorry."

"I appreciate you being straightforward, Mr. Hanson. If Sheriff Pruett trusts you, so do I." The young man looked over at Pruett. "I'll be okay. Hell, it's warmer in here and I get three meals a day. Sounds cliché, but when you're hungry, it's just a damned nice thing."

Hanson checked his watch. "We've got a few minutes. I want to present a couple of options. Nothing has to be decided now, but if you're going to be in here, at least you can use the time to think things over. First, I want you to see a doctor I know—"

"A shrink."

"A *medical doctor*. A psychiatrist."

"That's a shrink, Mr. Hanson."

"You had to see one when they let you out of the Army, didn't you?"

"Yeah. For all of ten minutes."

"That's exactly why I want you to see this man. He's written four books on PTSD."

"You want to tell them I did it because I was crazy when I don't believe I did it at all?"

"No, I want to find out *why* you don't remember. If we can figure out a way to bring back your memories of that night, wouldn't you want to? You said yourself if you *did* commit these crimes, you'd want to take responsibility."

"Whoa, there, Professor," said Pruett. "Kyle didn't kill those men."

"That's what all of us here believe. But to walk into the courtroom with 'I don't remember' isn't going to amount to a defense. In fact, it will almost *insure* a conviction. Four counts."

The three sat in silence.

"When would I have to do this?"

"Kyle—"

"No, Sheriff. Didn't you say you trust Mr. Hanson?"

"I did."

"Then *we* trust him. If we were in the war zone, you think Mr. Hanson should trust you or me? Or would he be better off trusting himself? This is *his* area of expertise."

Pruett nodded.

"Set it up," Yoder said. "I'll see a whole *team* of shrinks if you want me to."

Pruett asked Hanson if there were any way he could give him some time alone with Kyle. The attorney thought about it and said he'd tell the deputy outside he forgot something in the car. He said they usually gave him an hour with his client. Or more, if he needed it. Most of the deputies felt a lot of respect for Yoder, regardless of what happened after coming home.

~

"I want to talk about that day," said Pruett.

"You know it's classified, Sheriff."

"Speaking of knowing things, you're aware I'm not sheriff anymore."

"For a guy like you, being sheriff isn't a job—it's not an elected thing— it's who you are at your core. Just like I always knew I wanted Delta. You are who you are."

"Tell me about what happened that day. It's me; don't feed me any of that classified horseshit. What's said in here stays in here."

"Yeah, I guess you can be trusted," Yoder said.

And he started talking.

"The expert in battle
seeks his victory
from strategic advantage
and does not demand it
from his men."

~ Sun Tzu

Chapter 10

YODER LISTENED in his headset to the brief affirmation from the 4th BCT—Brigade Combat Team—82nd Airborne Division, boots on the ground—call for assistance. Not just assistance, but *Mayday*. The 4th BCT were known as Task Force Mountain Warrior; if they called emergency, it had to be a no-joy situation—beyond the control of one elite unit of men.

Mayhem.

The call had come in at the secret FOB where Yoder and his group of Deltas counted out the days, waiting for just this type of rescue mission. Delta teams had internal, classified names, so the hunter-killers, as they liked to call themselves, put nicknames to the various groups of steely young patriots, each member willing to risk the greatest gift he'd ever be given—for a cause; for a country; even for countrymen and women who hated them. Yoder's team was Spiderman, which was fine by him as his grandfather had bequeathed an entire collection of comic books from the 70s, most of them Spiderman, and Yode *loved Spiderman*.

"Copy your sitrep," said Colonel Stanton, team commander. "Team Spidey is two minutes from bird in the air. We're coming to get you."

Colonel Jeremiah Stanton. By far the most terrifying individual Yode had ever *imagined* could exist. The commanding officer had spent more time in the blood and mud than their entire team combined; he'd been cut, shot, beaten, tortured, broken, stitched, and put back together so many times he resembled a Frankenstein monster of sorts.

With a personality to match.

But you'd have a tough time finding a more hellacious, *HOOAH*, hard-ass finder and killer of men to lead you into the shit.

He defined the kind of man who'd unlikely been born of any woman, suckling at anything as anthropological as a life-giving, nurturing breast, but rather was *conjured*, stomping out one day from the smoke and carnage of one battle or another—already battletested; already bloodied; already healed and ready for the next evolution.

Kyle admired his commander, but he feared him, too.

As it should be—as the leader of men willing to dispense hell should be no less than the Devil himself—so it was. Colonel Jeremiah Stanton might actually *be* Mephistopheles, but he was a necessary evil and he was on *Yode's* team.

~

"Sounds like a fucking psychopath," said Pruett.

"I think that's the first qualifier on the application for commander of a group of men whose duty is to go wherever no one else will, bucking twenty-to-one odds, out-gunned, on foreign soil, and the best odds of success being 50/50."

"Good point."

"Look, I never liked the guy—no one did—but his job wasn't Camp Counselor or Troop Leader. I've still yet to meet a more kick-ass, take names, and do-it-all-again-tonight kinda guy. If anyone's going to get you through it, Stanton would.

"Tell me the rest," said Pruett.

~

The land in southwestern Afghanistan, had there not been all that dying going on, would have impressed all the men, most of all Yoder, growing up so close to the Rocky Mountains; visiting his godfather, James Pruett, in Wind River, hiking, climbing, fishing the transparent, icy waters of the rivers and lakes.

But there *was* all that dying going on.

So now all that lay before him as he descended his drop rope, silently, as always ready for this to be his last day on earth, was hell. Steep, jagged terrain, an enemy who always held the high ground, deadfall that could kill you itself if you fell into it, boulders that could dislodge and pin a man's foot or entire leg, leaving him the option of sawing it off, eating a bullet, or waiting for the enemy to eventually find him, and do things far worse than sawing.

So because of all the danger and death, the surrounding area wasn't beautiful, majestic, or picturesque at all. It was just land. Area. Coordinates. Until they were in it; then it was simply the next fight. Life or death was not a cliché used by those in Spec Ops. They'd long since learned such were the definitive ends of the spectrum on which they lived, trained, fought, played, and believed.

It was nature's own gladiator arena, and death would always be around them, above and below, around a corner, over the next hill—in the very air they took in with controlled, adrenaline-suppressing breaths.

The most difficult thing for the men and women in Special Forces to learn was not the endurance of fatigue and pain, nor was it to control their fear—in truth, both fear and physical pain became milestones by which to measure themselves, and because of which they knew they were still alive. It was to lower the body's own chemical and physical reactions to the battle zone; a place that could never be fully feigned or recreated in the training fields.

When you had to keep your calm and wits about you when people were dying, some by your own hand, others compatriots, next to you, ahead or behind you—friends with nicknames and places in your heart—that was when the intense practice and physically and mentally controlling the reactions of the body paid off.

The second of two 82nd BCT's pilots had become disoriented when his sister helo had exploded in front of him, hit by a Surface-to-Air Missile, or SAM, blood and insides flying backward into the near-silent turbines of his own bird, causing her to rear and buck like a saddle bronc in a Friday night rodeo. By the time the pilot had executed an extraordinary recovery—one that would earn him a posthumous medal of uncommon valor, landing the bird, hard, killing four crew members and dying himself, but saving eight.

Still, what remained of 82nd was some unknown number of clicks off course. And as fate would decide the day, the chopper had crashed into the bottom of a crevasse with near vertical walls of granite climbing skyward in a tight "V", leaving the survivors pinned without cover and without means of escape.

Most of the remaining eight Rangers were either injured, in a condition of trauma shock, or both.

Lost. Disoriented. Scared.

The mission had been to quietly insert themselves in the craggy mountain terrain below the Afghan tree line, two units surrounding the position of a high value target believed to be using the elevated ground to move between several sniper nests, killing Allied forces in the region below, and to take out the man.

Two-dozen soldiers meant to encircle the infamous sniper, Emal Khan Ahmadzai. It may have seemed too many resources for the takedown of one combatant, but Ahmadzai was doing enough damage to friendly forces to have climbed high on the list of valued targets; high enough to warrant such an operation.

But now the silent approach was not only completely dead—the remaining chopper crew were now almost totally uncovered, with only the crumpled hull of the helo as protection.

And above them, somewhere, Emal Khan Ahmadzai, the Nine of Spades, would pick them off one by one, at his leisure, unless the rescue mission could somehow extract them.

The CIA knew Ahmadzai better than he knew himself. Literally. They had found a history that had eluded Emal Khan all his life. Where his parents were killed and why; his actual place of birth; his given name, Mirwais Khan.

But none of that mattered much to the CIA, and *not a shred* of it mattered to either the 82nd or Team Spidey. They were both on the away team's field, facing the best player on their squad, and nothing ended until the 82nd soldiers were extracted, picked off by the enemy, or the sniper was dead.

Colonel Stanton gathered the ground team after the ropes were extricated and the unit was boots on the ground. The chopper had flown to waypoint Oscar and would act on the next orders.

"This is what we train for, men," the colonel said.

Seven nods answered him.

"When things go to shit, that's when we do our best work," he continued. "Trig, I want you, Gaston, and Ham to climb toward that tall rock, the one with the three trees. If I was to pick a spot, that middle tree has excellent vantage and protection of the other pair. If you can make it that far—to the target—you have the green light; take him out. In fact, here's a standing order: Ahmadzai is green-lit, period. Do not—I repeat, *DO NOT* wait for confirmation to kill.

"Trig, if full approach is not possible, get as close as you can and be in position for cover fire. Wait for the order. Keep your butts *down*; consider us at full disadvantage in present positions. And don't forget how good this guy really is. This is 'no shit' time. GO."

Trig, Gaston, and Ham moved soundlessly into the dark, infrared goggles and scopes engaged.

"Breaker, Severide, and Dutch: Same plan as the other three, but take that far ridge. See the 'U' shape where the ridge dips down, maybe eight feet off the ground?"

Three nods.

"Secondary position. Perfect elevation, cover, and another pure line of sight to the downed chopper in the gorge. Same orders. If you can't find Ahmadzai, get close, butts down, and wait for the order to lay down cover fire. GO."

And as the second trio moved away without even the snap of a broken branch, it was Colonel Stanton and Yode.

"We're going to flush this bastard out," said Stanton.

"Yes, sir."

~

Pruett shook his head. "Impossible odds. That's what they trained you for."

"Yep. But every last one of us signed up for it."

"Well what was Stanton's plan to bring this killer out into the daylight?"

"That's where he and I disagreed," said Kyle. "I saw a glint in the center of the tree line. Above. Less cover, and more to the middle of the ridge, but the intel on Ahmadzai was pretty specific—he preferred better ground to cover. I told the colonel it was a better vantage point but he felt his assessment was correct.

"He wanted the two of us to take to the east—what he considered to be the secondary sniper nest—but he wanted me to use my rock-climbing skills to scale the granite cliff that would bring me out below Ahmadzai's lower peripheral line of sight but right beneath him. Stanton would go wide, through the forest, and once I'd radioed I was in position, would cause a distraction that would cause Ahmadzai to focus on the eastern ridge. I was to come at him from below and go for the silent, hand-to-hand kill."

"Jesus," said Pruett.

"Yeah, I didn't like the plan for a couple reasons. One, that's not where he was. Two, we already had a pair of teams coming up the east *and* west side of the crevasse where the 82nd was pinned."

"So you took to the rock face?"

"There wasn't time. Stanton took off into the forest and he couldn't have been gone a minute when the whole eastern slope of trees exploded like a, orange cloud of fire the size of Wisconsin."

"Claymores?" said Pruett.

"Or C-4," Kyle said. That whole tree line was booby-trapped."

"And the colonel?"

"Stanton was dead. Shit, I saw the bottom half of his left leg come flying through the air.

"I called to the other guys. No one had reached Ahmadzai. So I told them about the explosive ambush and Stanton's death. That put Severide in charge, so I cleared it with him for me to climb for a higher position on the center nest, where I saw the light reflection. To me a bit of hoofing it, but when I got up high, I could see Ahmadzai was in those trees. I had to flush him out.

"On my signal, the rest of the team laid down cover fire at the two nests Colonel Stanton had identified, as previously planned. I hoped when Ahmadzai saw the mistake, his ego would force an errant move. When the gunfire started going off, the target leaned a bit forward. I could see the bastard smiling, watching the Delta boys firing at the wrong targets.

"He gave me enough. It was a kill shot any of our guys and most the Rangers and Berets I know could have easily made. Not enough for any medals of valor."

Pruett put his hand on Kyle's shoulder. "That's not why you got the medals. I saw the report. You climbed down into the crevasse and pulled those injured Rangers out one by one, even after Taliban reinforcements arrived."

"Yeah," Kyle said. "Turned out Ahmadzai had a radio and called for more guns before I popped him."

"Report said you took a backboard down for each of the injured and when humping it back to the chopper, returned twice after Ham and Trig went down. Carried them *and* the Rangers on the backboards. Fifty yards of uncovered ground to the helicopter," Pruett said, beaming.

"That's when I lost my knee," said Kyle.

"That's when you saved three more lives."

"Court will come to order," the heavyset bailiff said. "All rise for the Honorable Judge Milford Cain." The entirety of the room rose as one and, from behind the bench, a door could be heard to open and close, but there was no judge. Not for a few silent moments, anyway.

Hanson held back a smirk. Judge Cain was a well-respected judge in the Ninth Circuit, with a reputation for three things:

1) A tendency to be a bit hard of hearing; the rumor being that he refused all manner of hearing aid devices.

2) Being a fair judge, who understood the law as well as any who'd ever sat and presided over a trial. And:

3) Being the shortest circuit court judge in the history of civilized law.

The diminutive magistrate made his way up the steps to his seat, the first part of him that came into view being his bald pate, ringed by frizzy white hair. He was not technically a dwarf—or little person—but his height was estimated somewhere *below* the five-foot mark.

The judge himself had never said, and probably never would, but Hanson had met the man in person twice and didn't believe he was a mark above four and a half feet.

"Sit, sit," the elder judge said, and the courtroom obliged. "We're just back from a half-hour recess, working through a busy morning docket. Since we are on time, I suggest we keep moving. Bailiff Swanson?"

"Call case number eight-four-four-seven-nine. State versus Kyle Vincent Yoder."

Maggie Forster was already at the prosecutor's table. Hanson waited at the defendant's. A door opened in the rear of the courtroom and Kyle was led to stand next to his lawyer.

"Madame Prosecutor," said Cain.

"Please the court, Your Honor, Maggie Forster representing the People."

Cain squinted down to see the tall, reedy defendant's attorney. "J.W. Hanson," the old judge said warmly. "Your credentials precede you. However, I don't believe I've had the pleasure of presiding over a case with you in my court."

"No, Judge. I don't think I've ever been in your court before."

"Well it's good to see you here now. You and I can pose for a picture later," he said, drawing light laughter from an otherwise tense crowd. "I assume you represent the defendant."

"Yes, Your Honor."

"Good. Well, Ms. Forster, when you are ready you may proceed with the reading of the charges."

"Thank you, Your Honor. The State does charge the defendant, Kyle Vincent Yoder, with four counts of capital homicide and four counts of hate crime ending in homicide."

"Mr. Yoder," Cain said, addressing the stunned defendant. "Do you understand the charges as read to you?"

"No, sir—uh, Your Honor—"

Hanson bent over and whispered in Kyle's ear.

"But what's the *hate crime* thing?" Kyle whispered a bit too loudly, to Hanson.

"Your Honor, a moment to confer with my client, if you please."

"Granted."

Hanson spoke as quietly as possible. "Kyle, I told you about this. It's process only. Just say you understand."

"But I *don't* understand. What is this stuff about hate crimes?"

"The victims were gay. The D.A. is elected. She's making a point to her constituency."

"I don't *hate* anyone. And certainly not gay—homosexuals. I have attended rallies; one of my best friends from high school was gay—"

"And *all* of this will be testified to at trial."

"Mr. Hanson, is there an issue?" said Judge Cain.

"No, Your Honor. One more moment." Hanson looked back to Kyle. "Remember what you said about trust? *Trust me.*"

Kyle looked like an animal that had lost its way and ended up in a crowded park of strangers. "All right. All right. Whatever has to be done."

Hanson turned back. "My apologies to the Court, Judge."

"May we continue?" Cain said.

"Yes."

"Fine. Mr. Yoder. Do you understand the charges as read to you?"

"Yes, Your Honor."

"And how do you plead, sir?"

"Not guilty, Your Honor."

"Fine. Thank you, Mr. Yoder. Are there any other pending motions or matters before the Court?"

"Request bail, Your Honor." Hanson said.

"Sorry, can you speak up, Mr. Hanson?"

"Request bail for my client, Your Honor."

"Well, yes, but you know I can't grant bail in a capital murder case."

"With all due respect, Your Honor, under law you are granted the final say in such matters. My client is a recipient of the Congressional Medal of Honor. He has no criminal record, his entire family lives in the community—"

"I'm sorry, Mr. Hanson. The Court thanks you for your meritorious service, young man. Bail, however, is denied. The defendant is remanded." The judge looked down for a few moments at his calendar. "I'd like to move this trial as quickly as possible. Ms. Forster and Mr. Hanson, I think two weeks is sufficient and fits well with the Court's calendar. If there are no objections, I set trial date for nine A.M. on Wednesday, August 3rd."

"No objection, Your Honor," said D.A. Forster.

"No objection, Judge," said Hanson.

"Good." Judge Cain banged his gavel. "Next case."

Sloan Martin was at her desk at noon when Sri knocked on her door. She waved him in. "Good work on the website. I want you to thank the whole team. You've been keeping up with the story; the coverage has been excellent—what?"

Sri held out a piece of printer paper. "I found this story a little while ago. The search algorithms spewed it out. I almost tossed it with the rest of the older news we already have."

Sloan read the story, dated shortly after the veteran's parade that had honored Kyle Yoder. The story was from a conspiracy site known for its crackpot reporting, and purported to be the tale of how Kyle Yoder won his Medal of Honor.

"They claim the details of the story are real—the source leaked a classified document," Sri said. Sloan gave him the *you've-got-to-be-kidding-me* look. "I know, I know, but I started checking into it. I cross-referenced some other stories, bits here, bytes there. Did you read the part at the end about his commanding officer—a Colonel Jeremiah Stanton?"

"Yeah. Says Yoder reported he was killed by an explosive ambush but the body was never found. The Army assumed one of the Taliban tribes in the area either desecrated his dead body or captured him and killed him."

"Thing is, it's true. I mean the part about Stanton being M.I.A. I found an official public report of casualties."

"Okay, so the kid guessed wrong. The mine didn't kill his commanding officer, the Taliban did."

Just then, Sloan's assistant came in with a strange look on her face. "There's a call parked for you. It's a woman and she's crying."

"Where?"

"I'll transfer her to your primary line."

A few moments later, the phone rang and Sloan picked up. "This is Sloan Martin."

"P-please. I couldn't think of anyone else to call. Please help me…"

"Calm down, uh, who is this?"

"Allison. My name is Allison."

More quiet sobbing.

"Allison, I want you to listen to me. Are you in danger right now? If you are, you need to dial 911."

"I can't call 911. The Army man might answer. He already killed—"

The girl named Allison began crying harder and seemed to have put down the phone. Sloan tried her name several times but couldn't get a response. She hit the mute button. "Sri, can you trace this girl's phone call?"

"Not unless you have her call your cell, or know someone *really* well at the phone company. Your office line is still on the old PBX system."

"Sloan?" Allison called into her earpiece.

She unmuted her phone. "I'm here, Allison." Sloan tried the phone again.

"I don't want to die…"

"No one is going to die, okay? But I don't want you to put your phone down anymore. I want you to promise."

"Okay."

"Say you promise."

"I promise I won't put the phone down."

"And you need to stay calm."

"I'm scared."

"I understand," said Sloan. "But if you don't stay calm, I can't help you. That's why you called me, right? To help?"

"Yes. You've been writing about the murders."

"About the Army man," Sloan said.

"Nooooo," Allison bawled.

"Allison, I said calm—down."

"They don't have the Army man. The police let the Army man kill my parents."

"Okay, Allison, I need to ask you: are you taking any medication or have you been drinking?"

"No. I'm h-hiding."

"From the Army man?"

"Yes."

"What's your last name, honey?"

"Chapman."

"Allison Chapman?"

"Yes."

"Where do your parents li—where is your parent's house, Allison?"

"On Cherry Street."

"Where on Cherry Street, Allison? Are you at your parent's house?"

"I don't know where I am…he killed them. He's looking for me because I saw what he did."

"Don't move. Stay where you are." Sloan hit mute again. "I think I have a crazy person on the line. Or a possible drug overdose in the making."

A reporter came running into Sloan's office, pushing right past Sri.

"Sorry, Sri. Sloan, you're going to want to hear this—NOW. The police scanner just came alive. There's a double homicide over on Cherry Street."

> "Dreams are often most profound
> when they seem the most crazy."
>
> ~Sigmund Freud

Chapter 11

KYLE YODER lay still on his back on (what passed for) a couch at the county detention center. Hanson had scheduled Dr. Emil Weiss to come up from Fort Collins, Colorado, where his old friend had a practice.

Weiss was not only a recognized expert in the study of Post-Traumatic Stress Disorder—PTSD—but was also a licensed hypnotherapist who had seen remarkable results regaining memories in many of his trauma patients.

When Hanson had first suggested the idea of hypnosis, both Pruett and Yoder had nearly fired him on the spot. Trust with those two seemed to be a tenuous proposition. But Hanson persisted. He explained that modern procedures were actually sanctioned by the American Medical Association *and* the American Psychiatry Association and were far different from the huckster methods and frauds of decades past.

Dr. Weiss had the lights turned down, a light ambient music in the background, and was speaking to Yoder in soft, pleasing tones.

"Just close your eyes, Kyle. I want you to do your best to separate yourself from the current surroundings, relax, and try to let the stress drain from each muscle, tendon, out your pores.

"Imagine the place you are, your current position in reality, as only one of many places along the timeline of your life. Try to see your existence as if on a long line where you are able to traverse from now back into your military training or a high school dance. No limitations. For now, you are free."

Kyle felt the stress, the worry, and the feelings of constant fear melting away. He'd not thought such an experience anything more than hocus pocus, but he had decided, as always, never to enter anything he was going to do without his positive, can-accomplish mentality. He was going to put everything into this and see what came out the other side.

"I want to take you to a place on your life-line, Kyle. Back to an evening a few nights before. But I want you to go further back than anything out of the ordinary. Find a moment or a common, comfortable feeling from that evening. Perhaps a meal or a moment of beauty you noticed. Anything that brought you happiness from that evening."

Kyle floated back in his mind to the night in question. Back to the light, early in the evening, before dusk, when he was relaxing as he often did with his guitar and his music. He was far from the commotion on Front Street, where he could do what he liked. In fact, the commotion on the other side of the building behind which he lived provided a cover for his own musical ventures.

He was no professional singer, but Kyle had written a few songs—some before he joined the Army, some while training at Fort Benning, others while deployed, even, although those melodies were kept mostly in his head. Sometimes he would scrawl some lyrics in his journal.

But that night, the air was warm but a nice, cooling breeze wafted back into the alley. And as the sun went down, he remembered a magnificent glow of reds and blues and purples in the lightly clouded sky.

It was as perfect a night as Kyle had spent back at his home, Cheyenne, and he felt the hope of that night wash over him again—hope of returning to his family one day; hope of visiting Wind River, and his friend and father, Sheriff Pruett.

He'd not come back to Wind River after Aunt Bethy's death—too much grief had consumed him; but in not going, he'd missed those one of a kind Wind River night skies—and for once the glow of the Cheyenne city lights was dampened and the beautiful nighttime filled him so with hope that he got out the guitar and played a few of the old regulars he knew by heart—some covers from other bands; others, songs he'd written himself—nothing too heavy. Just peaceful music, on a peaceful night.

It was then the memory of the four men came back to him. They had stumbled out the rear of the bar instead of the front, obviously intoxicated—as was ninety percent of the partiers downtown that night.

The four of them, dressed nicely in jeans and western boots, and sports jackets, had drifted over toward the sound of his playing. Kyle was not particularly social, except when he played. When he played his guitar, and the music took grasp of his soul, he became more of the young, hopeful dreamer he'd always been; Kyle Yoder, who always set his sights high and always achieved his dreams.

The men were appreciative of his playing and for fifteen or twenty minutes Kyle had almost felt as if in concert. The four men would clap politely, or even cheer a little, and Kyle would break into another tune.

Just five guys, enjoying Frontier Days. As it had been in the good old—

A frown creased his face. He stopped playing. One of the men had suddenly choked on the food he'd brought or—wait—it was blood, leaking from the man's mouth. Then a second of the men was knocked hard to the ground with a glancing blow. By then, the two remaining upright were fighting with—*someone*.

Kyle instinctively tossed the guitar and jumped to their aid. First helping the downed man but then reaching through the mass of bodies—blood flowing, more and more—and, he realized, they were losing the fight; a fight against whom he had not yet known, which made gaining the upper hand impossible. Another of the men dropped to the ground, barely conscious, his jugular cut wide open, blood pumping out in a stream, rhythmically with the man's waning heartbeat. Then, as the last standing victim spun sideways, Kyle saw the assailant.

It. Was. Him.

The monster in his dreams.

The scarred, burned, mutilated face that seemed too inconceivably outrageous to be real, and yet—those eyes. He'd seen those eyes before. Never in his dream—in his dreams, there was only the hideousness; nothing as human as eyes.

But this time it was *not* a dream.

Dark gray, emotionless eyes, one nearly cut out, a scar running from above the left eyebrow down, disappearing as it crossed the eye socket, then picking back up in line with the originating arc, and continuing down the left cheekbone until it disappeared in a mass of burned, deformed flesh.

Those eyes—the lifeless, merciless eyes of the shark—locked with Kyle for just a moment, sunken in a face that was a mass of molten horror, and then the owner returned to butchering the final two men.

Kyle bolted upright on the couch, sweating profusely, ice cold.

Terrified.

Pruett's phone rang. It was a number he did not recognize—only the 307 Wyoming prefix.

"Pruett."

"James Pruett? Sir, this is Sloan Martin at the *Tribune Eagle*."

"Yes, ma'am. I've read many of your stories. Big fan."

"I appreciate that, Mr. Pruett."

"James, please."

"James, then. I'm sorry to bother you, but Chief Wallace gave me your number. When I reported my investigative findings to him, his exact words were 'this is Sheriff James Pruett's investigation.' He essentially told me you had the full backing of the Cheyenne Police Department and that I should tell you what I know."

Pruett was silent for a moment in disbelief. Earlier in the day he was negotiating with a violent, murderous felon—a felon and treasured friend; now he was once again Sheriff James Pruett, if only—and unofficially—for a short time. "What can I do for you, Ms. Martin?"

"Sloan. Please. And I have a woman on the other line I believe your team is searching for. Allison Chapman?"

"Do you know where she is?"

"Not at the moment. Are you aware that several hours ago—"

"Yes," Pruett said. "I'm sorry for interrupting. I know what happened to her parents."

"As you can imagine, I don't want to release any of this news to the public and incite a panic. It seems we still have a murderer on the loose."

"That's why I'm a fan, ma'am—uh, Sloan. You are intelligent as well as talented."

"What can I do to help?"

"First, is there any way you think Ms. Chapman might call *me*?"

"It's worth a try. Give me a minute."

Pruett waited, impatiently. Earlier Red Horse had filled him in on Allison Chapman's boyfriend, and the words he had said she kept repeating:

The Army dude killed those men.

"Sheriff Pruett?" said Sloan Martin.

"Here. Sorry. I was contemplating a lead."

"I talked her into calling you. But you are *not* a member of law enforcement. This is key to her. She's in a state of shock and believes the Army man is part of the police department. Or teamed with them somehow. The poor girl doesn't know who to trust. I told her you weren't even *from* Cheyenne—that you were from Wind River—and that seemed to help."

"Why is she so paranoid?"

"She is convinced that 'the Army man' killed her parents and is with the police because, well, I'm not sure—because they both wear uniforms, maybe? She said they have the wrong man. I was about to dismiss her as a crackpot when the police scanner picked up the murders at the Chapman house."

"When she calls, who am I?"

"You are my most trusted reporter, and you will bring her in to me and me only. That's my promise to her."

"Tell her you're coming, too. I'm going to need someone who knows Cheyenne. I'll be at The Paisley House. Do you know where that is?"

"Yes. I'll tell her to call you right away. I should be there to meet you in ten minutes."

Pruett waited for what seemed five minutes, when his phone actually rang. He looked skyward and said a silent prayer of thanks to God and Bethy.

"Hello."

"Is this Mr. Pruett?"

"Yes, young lady. Is this Allison?"

"Yes."

"Listen, Sloan and I want to come get you and bring you to safety. Can you help me figure out where you are?"

"I think they call it the Waterfront District. It's by the river, I know that. I can smell the fish and hear the water splashing against the boards."

"Anything else, dear?"

"There's a red light flashing outside. Up high, maybe on the roof. It goes off every few seconds. I don't know what it is, though. And Mr. Pruett? My cell is almost out of juice. Don't let the Army man get here first."

"The Army man isn't going to hurt you, okay sweetie? Don't move. We're coming for you."

~

While he was waiting for Sloan, Pruett's cell rang again. "Pruett."

"We've had a breakthrough," Hanson said, as if he could barely keep his voice down. "Kyle remembers what happened. It was his colonel he saw that night. The monster in his dreams. He also remembers the murders at the alleyway that night. It was Stanton."

"We've found Allison Chapman," Pruett said. "I think she witnessed the whole thing, too. But if we know where she is—"

"Go," said Hanson. "I'm going to go share our new information with Maggie Forster."

~

A few minutes later Pruett was standing in front of The Paisley House on the curb when a white Volvo pulled up and rolled the passenger window down. "Sheriff?"

Pruett bent and got in. "The Waterfront District she thinks. Down by the river where she can smell the fish."

"Cannery Row, people sometimes call it. Our girl just has her movies mixed up. Sloan, by the way, *officially*." She extended a smooth, slender hand and Pruett shook it, lightly.

Sloan worked her way up and out of the city and jumped on Interstate-25. "We should get there in ten, fifteen minutes."

"I got a call from Kyle's attorney. They decided to try some kind of memory reenactment or hypnosis or something. Anyway, I guess it worked. He remembers seeing his old colonel there, the night of the murders."

"Colonel Stanton."

"That's right. How did you—"

"You wouldn't believe it. The luck of a writer on a deadline. An old conspiracy website story we found reported that Colonel Stanton was *not* killed in combat, as Sergeant Yoder thought. Apparently, he was taken in by a family or some friendlies, who nursed him back to health. Then he must have made his way back to the States, undetected. The military assumed the absence of the body meant either desecration or capture by the Taliban. Either way, same basic result. No body."

~

The pair exited I-25 at Riverfront Avenue and took a right on that street. As they reached a string of mostly unused warehouses, closed down in the recession, Pruett scanned for the light. "She said there was a constant flashing red light. Every couple of seconds."

"Any building in town higher than three stories is required to have a flashing light to warn planes."

"Then we're looking for—"

"THERE," Sloan said, pointing to a tall building—the only one with an aircraft warning light atop it. They stopped and got out. Pruett removed his revolver. There wasn't any reason to believe that Stanton was on to them, or the girl, but Allison had come down to that building for a reason—and if anyone else knew why she might come down there, Stanton could know.

"Maybe you should wait with the car," Pruett said.

"I feel safer with you," she said, her arm slung through his non-pistol hand.

"Not an unfair point."

They eased into the building, trying to be as quiet as possible.

"You're LATE, Sheriff," a voice called from the darkness.

"Stanton?"

"I have to say, I'm impressed with you and your deputies' small town police work. The Cheyenne PD doesn't seem to be able to get out of their own way."

"We just caught a couple of breaks. And without Sloan here, we'd probably never have gotten to adding two and two."

"Yes," said Stanton from somewhere in the warehouse. "I didn't count on Allison here having the wit to call someone who might *believe* her crazy story about the 'Army man.' But chance rolls funny. Different every day."

"You talk like a gambler," said Pruett.

"You can't be in Special Forces and not be a risk-taker. Gambling is a game of risk."

"It's a game of *chance*. That's the problem with you Spec Ops guys. All brawn, no brain."

"This from the man who turned down the Soldiers Medal."

Pruett was moving toward the voice, trying to pin down the location.

"Man's honor isn't measured by the weight of his medals," Pruett said.

"Is that what you did? The honorable thing?"

"What would you call traveling all the way to Cheyenne, Wyoming to frame and disgrace a boy who was twice the soldier you were?"

"It could still work. My plan."

"You can't have a body count with the prime suspect behind bars, nut bag."

"You should watch who you insult, friend."

"Not your friend, Stanton. Give me the girl. Let's end this thing the right way. These are all American citizens, not the enemy. There's no heroism in cold-blooded murder."

The man stepped into the light with the girl, knife to her throat. "She'd bleed out in less than a minute," Stanton said.

"You're a coward," Pruett growled.

"No, this is just the *brain* part of me deciding how I'd like the rest of this to play out."

"Well I'm sure you'll keep us all informed as you go through your thinking process."

"Originally, the Chapmans—the parents *and* lovely strung-out Allison here; who would make a terrible witness, by the way—were going to simply disappear. Then you and your deputies showed up before I could lay down the accelerants and get a real nice suburban barbeque going."

"Only one," said Pruett.

"Only *what*?"

"Only one of the men who showed up with me is a deputy. And neither of them is *my* deputy. Got dis-elected a few months back."

Ouch.

"Yeah, well, you roll with life's jabs just like you roll with the hooks and uppercuts." *Keep him talking; as long as he's talking, he's not slicing.*

"A boxing metaphor. Cliché, but appropriate. Did you do any boxing?"

"In the Army."

"See, I was thinking about the various outcomes for this cluster-fuck—being that you all have my name now, etcetera. I thought it might be fun for you to fight me for the lives of these two women here," Stanton said. "You said so yourself. My plan failed, I'm toast. You think you're such a hometown hero. Let's decide it right here and now. You can be the stand-in for your absent Medal of Honor recipient."

"Your ego can't be that big, Colonel. So Kyle gets the ticker tape parade. Who gives a rat shit? Let the girl go."

"Oh, no, Pruett. You've got it all wrong. I didn't come all the way back here to ruin poor young Kyle's life because he won the medals and not me."

"Then what in God's name is this about?" said Pruett.

"I know it's been a while, but do you remember the Army's first rule of engagement?"

"No one gets left behind."

"That's goddamned right," barked Stanton, spittle flying off his dry, cracked lips. "No one gets left behind."

"They thought you were blown to pieces."

"No, no. Not *they*. Yoder. *He* was the one who told the rest of the team I was gone."

"He saw your leg come flying down the hill," said Pruett. "What was the boy supposed to think?"

"What the *DELTA* soldier was supposed to think is that someone might still be alive in those trees. What the *DELTA* soldier was supposed to think was 'fuck my own idea to climb up the draw, which my commanding officer nixed—I need to double-time it over to where the explosion blew off *half my colonel's fucking LEG* and see if I can find him up there.'"

"What is the second thing you teach a Delta soldier, Colonel?"

"What?"

"The second thing. After 'leave no man behind', what's the next thing you drill into a soldier's head."

"The needs of the many are far greater than the needs of one soldier. And that dying for your country, particularly when saving lives, is the greatest honor a member of Team Delta can reach."

"Seems to me that the numbers won the day, sir."

"The numbers won the day—"

"Eight Rangers and the rest of your Delta team were rescued that day, Colonel. Even with them counting you among the dead, that was a pretty good day."

"Except I didn't get the honor of dying for my country."

"Well you missed the funeral, but I attended, and you were honored and buried as a patriot of these United States."

Stanton stood there. He looked like an animal that had heard a sound it did not quite recognize.

"I-I used my anger to survive. I promised myself that I would avenge being left behind."

"But you were never left behind, sir. Those men *worshipped* you. If they'd thought for one second that you survived that catastrophic blast—if Kyle had not been witness to your *body part* ripped from its torso—do you really believe they would have left you there?"

Again, Stanton was silent.

He was staring at the ground, and when he pushed Allison Chapman toward Pruett and Sloan Martin, he did not look up.

"I have become that which I foreswore to defend *against*," the colonel said. "I have become that for which I hold contempt. I—a commander of 1st Special Forces Operational Detachment-Delta—have terrorized a United States citizen *on* U.S. soil and I have committed six cold-blooded murders against citizens of the nation I swore an oath to protect."

"Give me the knife, Colonel," Pruett said. "Let's get you the help you need."

"I find myself guilty of all charges," said Stanton, and reversed his BK7 Combat Utility knife and without hesitation buried it hilt deep just to the left of center in his chest.

Straight through the heart.

Pruett ran over while Sloan stayed a few yards away, trying to calm a shaking Allison. The ex-sheriff knelt down, put his gun back in his holster, and placed a hand on the colonel's shoulder. The knife was moving in concert with his heartbeat: erratic and slow.

Stanton opened his eyes. He was fixated on Pruett's sidearm.

"Nice revolver," Stanton managed. "Just like me to bring a knife to a gunfight."

"Try not to talk," said Pruett. Before him was an evil man, but he was also a soldier. And he had let the girl go.

As if he'd read Pruett's mind, Colonel Stanton said, "They call it a moment of clarity. I was diagnosed bipolar two weeks before our last gig. I never should have been over there, in the shit. Paperwork hadn't cleared Division yet."

"Is there anyone you want me to—" but Stanton was already shaking his head.

"Tell Kyle," the colonel said, and then exhaled his final breath

> "It is a man's own mind,
> not his enemy or foe,
> that lures him to evil ways."

~Buddha

Chapter 12

IT TOOK a bit of time—a few days of paperwork formalities, sworn statements, and forensics matching of Colonel Stanton's BK7 Combat knife, prints, hairs, and fibers found at the Chapman house—for the charges against Kyle Yoder to be fully dropped and for the young man to be released.

Pruett, Wendy, and Kyle's grandmother (who was still able to get herself around with the aid of a walker) were at the bottom of the courthouse steps as attorney Hanson couldn't lead his free client away from the jaws of the inequitable legal system fast enough.

There was hugging, and the shaking of hands, but it wasn't until the silence that the idea sank in that there was no one to really say, "well, let's get you home—you could probably sleep a week in your own bed."

Pruett stomped on the silence: "Here's what I was thinking. Lot of happenstance over the past eight or nine months—too much, really, for any man's mind to be forced to wrap its logic around. I'm embarrassed I didn't think of it sooner—and God knows we could have avoided all this mess if I had—but there is this big house of mine in Wind River, and all these acres to hike, and of course the hundreds of lakes and rivers to fish. Well, it's exactly the kind of peaceful place for a man to take some time away from everything and everybody and Kyle, I'd like you to mull it over some, certainly, but I think you should come to Wind River, stay in the guest house out on my place, and just decompress for as long as necessary."

Kyle looked into the eyes of his godfather, tears brimming both, and nodded.

"Got me a few things I want to clear up here with gramps and granny, and you got yourself a deal, Sheriff."

"That was a kind thing to offer," said Sloan Martin as she and Pruett walked through the park down on Front Street, near the water. "I can't imagine a better place or a better man with whom to spend time."

"Does that go for Kyle or anyone?"

"Well, I—I meant Kyle, of course, but—now look at me: the writer with her tongue tangled."

"I didn't mean to spring it on you," Pruett said. "We haven't known each other all that long, but it doesn't take long to figure out I'm a man who speaks his mind. That's not always a good quality."

"Am I being invited to visit Wind River?"

"Have you ever been there?"

"No. Actually, yes, but just to stop for gas. Some friends and I were going up to Jackson to go skiing at Teton Village and I believe we stopped at a place called the Mini Mart?"

"That would be the Trailside now. But I wouldn't say that counts as having seen all our wonderful town has to offer."

"I'm sure there's a lifetime worth of wonder I've yet to see. I know even driving through, it's spectacular. And I believe you owe me a dinner to boot."

"I owe *you* a dinner?"

"I think there is something deep in the police handbook that says any time a lead is officially brought to a law enforcement agent by a reporter, and that lead helps to break a case, said law enforcement agent owes said reporter dinner."

"I must've missed that one in the handbook. But I think it's a damn fine rule," said Pruett. Cat and mouse again. When he'd given up that game forty odd years earlier, he'd planned on it being for good.

"Like Kyle, I have some loose ends here. In fact, I should really be down at the *Tribune* getting the news on the wire. Funny thing is, the case broke so quickly, and the suspect, well, gave himself up, so to speak, that there's hardly a story to retract. And I spent the better part of the entire first night worried to death that the entire story would blow up and the *Tribune* would end up sucking hind tit."

"Now if *that's* not a Wyoming expression, I don't know what is."

Sloan had been so caught back up in the whirlwind of the past couple of days that it took a moment to realize what she'd said. "Ah, yes. Very ladylike."

"If it makes any difference, I approve."

"It *does* make a difference, James Pruett," Sloan said, slipping her arm inside his. "It most certainly does."

D.A. Forster was tidying up her office, a chore normally reserved for the aftermath of a loss in court. She hadn't lost, per se—and she didn't feel that way either, which was important. She had her aspirations, but convicting an innocent man—worse, putting him to death—was nowhere on her list of acceptable political maneuvers.

She was more upset that there wasn't a trial. Deciding to return to Cheyenne and work in the prosecutors' office had been a difficult one. Wyoming—even Cheyenne—was not the center of crime in the country, and though she didn't *wish* crime upon her hometown, the idea of standing up in criminal court and prosecuting a quadruple homicide had really gotten her blood pumping.

And if she were being honest, seeing Jay Hanson after all those—

"Just like law school," a voice from behind—Jay Hanson's voice—pronounced. "After every mock court loss, I knew I could find you cleaning your dorm room."

Maggie Forster had to delay a moment before turning around; her cheeks were flush with—what? Something, anyway. So she shuffled a few more papers and put a pile of law books back on the shelf before turning to face him.

"No gloating allowed on this one," Forster said. "This was a win-win."

"Agreed," said Hanson. "I only came by to say adieu before riding back into the west from whence I came."

Seeing Maggie Forster again—though he'd known she was in Cheyenne for years, if not decades, and could have come over the mountains a hundred times had he really wanted to—well, it still had him bundled up inside like a spring that had twisted inward on itself and was no longer capable of any movement whatsoever.

What made it worse was that Wendy had given no date to his question of marriage, which still made them fiancés, but begged the question on whether indefinite timelines were timelines at all.

Add to which Wendy had no idea at all about Maggie—that she and Hanson attended law school together, dated (if you could call six on-again/off-again sexual escapades dating), nor could she *possibly* know how he felt now, seeing Forster again, since Hanson could not answer that one for himself.

"Is that the only reason you returned," asked Forster coyly.

Hanson put his briefcase on the floor and walked around behind the D.A.'s large oak desk.

"Until this moment, I didn't know exactly *why* I came to your office before leaving." Without giving her a chance to respond, he swept her up in his arms and kissed her deeply. Maggie wrapped her arms around his neck and returned the advance, pushing her tongue deep inside Hanson's mouth.

It was like law school all over again. Hanson felt twenty.

The two of them pushed at papers and books on the desk, throwing them all to the floor. Clumsily Hanson fumbled with his belt and Maggie Forster hiked up her tight skirt and pulled down her sleek panties.

When Hanson entered her, they moaned in concert, as if they'd both been waiting for this very moment and hadn't known it. Hanson put his long, thin fingers on her shoulder blades and pulled her tight. Maggie Forster wrapped her long legs, still in heels, around his back and they made love as if it were the last day on earth.

~

When they had finished, uncomfortable silence owned the room. The two of them redressed, straightening up the office as they went along, neither willing—or capable—of speech.

Hanson finally decided to say something. *Anything.* "I've missed you very much."

"Thank you for saying that," Forster said, still not making eye contact. "I've missed you, too, Jay. But you're engaged."

"I am."

"I wish you weren't, if that helps."

"It doesn't, but it's good to hear."

"Why didn't you ever come over from Laramie? All those years—"

Hanson shrugged. "I've thought about that a lot these past forty-eight hours. At first, I was as bewildered as anyone. And then it hit me. I was afraid."

"Afraid?"

"That the long-legged, green-eyed, D.A. would have long since stopped waiting for the tall, awkward, retired trial lawyer teaching Law at the University of Wyoming."

"I could have come to Laramie. I heard you got married. I just assumed you still were."

"Didn't take," said Hanson.

"And now?"

"When Wendy is my current age, I'll be in diapers she'll be wanting to take ballroom dancing lessons."

"Diapers?"

"It was the first thing that came to mind."

"How much older are you?"

"She is my student. Twenty years. A few more than that."

"Do you *love* her?"

"Not the way I loved you."

"Yes, but no one is ever quite like your first real love."

"I love you still. Too, I mean. I didn't realize that until I kissed you. I need you to know something: whatever happens—whatever this ends up being—I did *NOT* come here nor consider what just happened as reckless or without feeling."

"I didn't either."

"As two attorneys, logical-minded, practical, good at weighing the facts and making tough decisions, I think we need to determine whether we consider this worth pursuing further—you and I, that is," said Hanson, *far* more lawyerly than he intended.

"I wouldn't have risked everything by making love to you on my desk with the door wide open if I didn't."

"I know."

"I still love you, too, Jay."

Pruett dialed the number he was given by Grinder.

"Yeah," from the other end.

"Looking for Grinder," Pruett said.

"JP," said Roberts. "Sorry for the clandestine crap. Too many other listeners. We don't even use phones anymore. Burners once in a while, but I didn't want us to have to talk on my personal line."

"Much appreciated," said Pruett.

"So where we at, Jimmy?"

"We found the real killer. Turned out to be a vendetta by his previous commander."

"Damn, that's some hardcore shit, even in the circles I travel. Brother putting brother in harm's way."

"Yeah, this guy—he was a colonel—he was all fucked up. Diagnosed with bipolar disorder *before* the team's deployment to Afghanistan."

"That's fucked up."

"Yep. Hoorah for the United States of Paperwork."

"So the kid's okay? They cut him loose?"

"Free and clear," said Pruett.

"And that eliminates the need for any other backup plans, yes?"

"Yes," Pruett said, having maybe never felt more happy to say that word. "But listen, Grinder, I don't want it to be like this. It was really good seeing you."

"Same here, Jimmy boy. And maybe we'll cross paths again. But you doin' what you do, and me doin' what I do, well, that just puts us on opposite teams. It ain't like football, though. We don't just get to leave it all on the field and shake hands. Believe me when I tell you, the kind of heat that's my constant companion, you don't want your name coming up as another trail down which these bastards will spend a million tax dollars hiking."

"Understood," said Pruett. "You just make sure you remember that the oath works both directions, compadre."

"That I will, JP. That I will. You get back to keepin' the law and order up there in God's country."

"Or something like that," said Pruett, and disconnected from Dillon "Grinder" Roberts, probably for the final time.

Epilogue

PRUETT'S CELL rang and he didn't recognize the number, but he enjoyed the ringtone for a moment—he'd finally figured out how to program a classic Willie Nelson jam into his smartphone.

"Hello—uh, Pruett."

"Hi, James," a woman's voice said.

Sloan Martin. Her voice had been haunting him for a while.

"Sloan. I'm halfway between nowhere and someplace in Wyoming, in the dark. Your voice is like that of the nightingale."

Good Christ, Pruett thought. He'd not used a line that cheesy since he baited a hook when he was a kid.

"Let me guess: halfway between Rawlins and Rock Springs."

"Pretty darn close, m'lady."

"M'lady, huh?"

Pruett hated the cat and mouse, tit for tat games.

"Just an expression" he said. "Not that you'd not be welcome—I mean, aw, shit. Excuse my French. Guy like me'd be lucky to be with a lady such as yourself. All class and brains, to boot."

"That's why I took to you, James. You're a man who says what's on his mind. I've known more than a few liars in my time."

"Well that's one thing I try never to do. Lyin' that is."

"Reason I am calling—other than I figured you'd be falling asleep about now and could use a distraction—is, well, you mentioned me coming up to Wind River. And the thing is, the *Tribune Eagle* does two or three sort of 'personal interest' pieces, where we devote a whole special section to a town in the state, interview a prominent person, such as yourself. It's a great way for residents of Wyoming to get to know their neighboring cities and towns better. I'd really love to come out and do a piece on Wind River. We bring a professional photographer, the works."

"And that's why you called," said Pruett, the deflation in his voice unintentional but hard to miss.

"The piece won't run for several months—we just did one on Cody. I could've waited until then to call. Plus, you still owe me that dinner."

Message received, five-by-five, thought Pruett.

"Sloan, *m'lady*, I'd love to show you around the majesty that is Wind River, Wyoming. You pick the dates. I'll work around your schedule since you're the big shot city gal."

"Ouch," she said.

"Nah, meant it as a compliment."

"Okay, then. I'll check out my work calendar, story lineup, our photographer's availability, etcetera. But let's plan on sometime over the next month or so."

"Works fine for me," said Pruett.

"Excellent," said Sloan. "May I call you next week?"

"You call anytime, Sloan."

"Well, thank you, James. Talk soon." And she disconnected.

Pruett stared out over the half-circle horizon and couldn't remember the last time he felt so at peace.

~

It wouldn't last. Pruett had just exited I-80 at Rock Springs and turned his truck north on highway 191, one hundred miles due north to Wind River. After thinking about Sloan, his mind had turned to the palpable silence in the truck between Wendy and Jay on the drive from Cheyenne to Laramie. He'd dropped them off at Hanson's Buckskin apartment with hardly a "thank you" or "see you soon" from either.

He hoped he hadn't done something to upset the two, but his instincts told him there was a rift between the two lovebirds. Such silences had a particular feel.

It was just after Pruett's truck cleared the glow of Rock Springs' city lights, driving him back into two-lane darkness, that his cell phone rang again.

"Pruett."

"Boss," said Red Horse Baptiste.

"Listen, Red Horse," Pruett scolded (far more good-naturedly than scolding), "I'm not sheriff anymore, so I ain't your boss either."

"Sorry, Pruett," said Baptiste. "I think when you hear the rest of this, you may find yourself wondering about that fact yourself."

"What's that supposed to mean? What's happened, Baptiste?"

There was a long, uncomfortable pause between satellite and space.

"I-I-just don't know how to say this," stuttered Baptiste.

Pruett's gut roiled. Red Horse Baptiste was the most resolute, unshakable man Pruett knew. If *he* was finding words difficult—

"Just be a cop, Red Horse," Pruett said evenly. "Tell me what the facts are, just like you've done a thousand times."

"Twenty minutes ago Melody came in to change out a dead shoulder mike. Light was on inside Sheriff Walker's office—he's not on duty. I mean, he *wasn't*. Not on the schedule."

"What's going on?" Pruett said. "Talk to me, Baptiste. It can't be that bad."

"Deputy Munney found the sheriff—he was slumped back in his chair."

"What?"

"It appears he killed himself, sir."

"Killed himself?"

"From the initial indications, he put the pistol under his chin, and pulled the trigger," said Baptiste.

Pruett drove in silence through the Wyoming night. "Nothing else out of order? No one else see anything? Heard anything?"

"Don't know yet, boss. This is just developing. I wanted to call you first."

"I'm glad you did, Deputy. You're the most professional cop I know, Red Horse. The situation—your team and the town—they're gonna need that more'n ever."

"Yessir."

"I'm still an hour and a half out. To hell with that," Pruett said, putting the pedal to the floor. "I'll be there in an hour. You secure that scene, like you've done countless times before; find out if there was anyone else in the building, interview 'em if they were. Send the gawkers back to the bars or, better, home. Make sure *no one* goes into that office until I get there. In fact, no one in the whole building. Tomorrow's Saturday anyway. That gives us a couple days to cover the scene from bottom to top. Lock it down."

"Yessir," said Baptiste again. He was clearly in shock.

"You got this, Deputy. A crime is a crime, even if it's against one's own person. Just stick to procedure. And your experience, Red Horse. Rely on that. This ain't your first dance."

"Understood, sir."

"I'll see you in an hour," Pruett said, and disconnected.

Pruett's gut roiled again for the second time in as many days.

Jake Walker was a lot of things, but he wasn't the type to take his own life.

On that, Pruett would bet his own.

ABOUT THE AUTHOR

R.S. Guthrie lives in Colorado with his beautiful wife, three Australian Shepherds, and a Chihuahua who believes she's a forty-pound Aussie. The Guthrie dogs are their children and there is no disputing the fact that the canines rule the household.

The author's next planned book is the third in the Detective Bobby Mac series, but somewhere in the near future, there is a dog book digging to get out, and it will pay homage to the kindest, most loyal animals on the planet.

Pictured here with the author is three-year-old Elsa. She is as intelligent and as beautiful as she appears (and knows it all too well.)

Other books by R.S. Guthrie

Sheriff James Pruett Mystery / Thrillers:

Blood Land
Money Land
Honor Land

Detective Bobby Mac Mystery / Thrillers:

Black Beast
L O S T
Reckoning

Non-Fiction:

INK: Eight Rules To A Better Book

www.ingramcontent.com/pod-product-compliance
Lightning Source LLC
Chambersburg PA
CBHW070331130626
46556CB00007B/2802